7330 c/n

DATE DUE

CT 8			
SL49			
FV 11			
BW5			

DEMCO 38-296

Books by Chrissie Loveday
in the Linford Romance Library:

REMEMBER TO FORGET
TAKING HER CHANCES
ENCOUNTER WITH A STRANGER
FIRST LOVE, LAST LOVE
PLEASE STAY AWHILE
A LOVE THAT GROWS
CONFLICT OF LOVE
FOOD FOR LOVE
OPPOSITES ATTRACT
SAY IT WITH FLOWERS
GROWING DREAMS
HIDDEN PLACES
TOO CLOSE FOR COMFORT
DOCTOR, DOCTOR
HOME IS WHERE THE HEART IS
CRANHAMS' CURIOS
ONLY A DAY AWAY
LOVE AT FIRST SIGHT
LESSONS IN LOVE

'I'LL BE THERE FOR YOU'

Amy returns home to find the house deserted and her father mysteriously absent. Her oldest friend Greg rallies round and they begin their mission to find her father. Had her father planned some sort of surprise holiday for her? Or was there a sinister purpose behind the mysterious phone calls? Mystery, adventure, possible danger and a trip to Southern Spain follow. But how could they enjoy the beautiful settings with such threats hanging over them?

CHRISSIE LOVEDAY

'I'LL BE THERE FOR YOU'

Complete and Unabridged

LINFORD
Leicester

First published in Great Britain in 2008

First Linford Edition
published 2009

British Library CIP Data

Loveday, Chrissie.
　'I'll be there for you' - -
　(Linford romance library)
　1. Fathers and daughters- -Fiction. 2. Missing
　persons- -Investigation- -Fiction. 3. Spain,
　Southern- -Fiction. 4. Love stories.
　5. Large type books.
　I. Title II. Series
　823.9'2–dc22

　ISBN 978–1–84782–758–6

Published by
F. A. Thorpe (Publishing)
Anstey, Leicestershire

Set by Words & Graphics Ltd.
Anstey, Leicestershire
Printed and bound in Great Britain by
T. J. International Ltd., Padstow, Cornwall

This book is printed on acid-free paper

Visit the author's website at:
www.chrissieloveday.com

An Empty House

The last leg of the journey seemed to be taking forever. Amy felt tired, grubby and in desperate need of some decent food and a nice drink. But Dad would be sure to have something organised; probably a takeaway ready to be delivered when she arrived and a decent bottle of wine chilling in the fridge.

She couldn't wait to see him. It had been almost a year since she'd gone to France, as part of her language course at university, and she had missed him terribly.

The train stopped for the umpteenth time in the middle of nowhere. She sighed, thinking the journey from Plymouth to Truro would never end. It was already half an hour late. Thank goodness she had told her father to wait at home. He would have been stomping up and down the platform, impatient and cross at being kept waiting. She planned to get a taxi home to save him the bother of collecting her.

'It'll be well worth it, darling,' he'd said on the phone before she'd left France. 'I'll pay for it when you get here. I'll have supper ready. We've got lots to catch up on. Some interesting stuff has come my way recently but I'll tell you all about it when we meet.'

At last, the train stopped in Truro station and the announcer said it was terminating there. All the passengers intending to travel on to Penzance were obliged to get off, and an angry babble broke out.

Amy escaped quickly and dragged her bags out to the first taxi in the rank, giving the driver her address, which was about twenty minutes away, in a small village close to the sea. They spoke briefly about the problems of travel, then she sat back, relaxing for the final stage of her journey.

'It's just along here,' she pointed out presently. 'The big house standing back on the left. Next one . . . this is it. You can easily turn in the drive. If you stop outside the front door, I'll call my dad. He's paying!'

'OK, love. I'll get your stuff out of the boot.'

'I can't think why there are no lights on,' she muttered almost to herself. 'He's expecting me. I thought he'd have put the outside lights on at least.'

Amy rang the bell to alert her father of her arrival and fished in her bag for her keys.

Something was stopping the door as she tried to push it open. She gave an almighty shove and reached for the light switch. There was a pile of letters behind the door.

'That's odd,' she muttered. 'Hello? Are you there, Dad?' she called.

'Something wrong, love?' asked the taxi driver as he dumped her bags down on the step.

'My dad seems to have gone out or something. And there's a mass of post behind the door. I don't understand it

— he knew I was coming.'

'I'm sorry, love, but the meter's still running — and I need to get on my way.'

'Oh, yes, of course — sorry. How much do I owe you?'

'Fifteen quid, I'm afraid.'

'Oh — right — hang on.' She scrabbled in her bag and just managed to collect fifteen pounds together from her various purses. She had some euros but hadn't yet drawn out any British currency.

'Sorry, that's all I've got — I've nothing left for a tip for you.'

'Not to worry. You can make up for it next time. I hope you find your dad all right.'

'Yes. I can't think what's happened to him. Goodnight, then. Thanks.'

Amy dragged her bags inside and shut the door, then picked up the mail to see if it would give her any clues. There was clearly at least three or four days' worth of envelopes and packages. Some was junk mail and she put that to

4

one side. There was something that looked like a book from a mail order company, a large packet with a solicitor's address stamped on the back, a couple more type-written envelopes, and a credit card statement. She put it all on the hall table and went through to the kitchen.

There was no welcoming smell of food cooking. There were a few dirty dishes in the sink and several coffee mugs littered the draining board. That was nothing new. Her father was often absent-minded when he was working on something and at times forgot about food entirely.

Coffee was different. There was always a pot of filtered coffee sitting on the side and he drank it black.

'Saves buying milk and watching it go sour,' he repeated every time she was home.

She touched the filter machine but it was quite cold. There were some dregs left in the bottom and the filter was stiff with old coffee grounds that had clearly been there for some days.

She emptied them into the waste bin and wrinkled her nose at the smell that arose. There was a collection of food in there that had gone off. However absent-minded her father, he was usually careful about throwing out the contents of the rubbish bin. She looked in the fridge. It was empty — completely cleared out.

'I don't understand this,' she muttered to herself. 'He definitely knew I was coming back today. I only spoke to him on Sunday.' Suppose he'd been taken ill? Or worse?

She gave a shudder and, steeling herself, went to look around the house. Her mother had died when she was a tiny baby, so she and her father had become very close, especially as she'd got older. Although she had been away and they had been apart for the longest time in her life, they had kept in touch all the time. They had sent emails to each other regularly and phoned at least once a week.

He usually worked from home, so his study was her first place to look. She switched on the light and peered round the door with some trepidation. His large desk was a mess — heaps of papers and books left open and piled on top of other books. There wasn't a space left empty, which was no different from his usual way of working. It looked exactly as though he had left the room to make some of his favourite coffee and would be back in a few minutes. She felt his computer, which was switched off and quite cold to the touch. Frowning, she glanced into the other downstairs rooms and then went upstairs. Each room was the same with no sign of life nor any clues as to where her father could be. In his bedroom his bed was made and the room looked remarkably neat and tidy.

It was all very strange, and so unlike her father to leave the place like this.

Downstairs again, Amy picked up the letters. Nothing special.

She tried hard to remember exactly

what he'd said the last time they'd spoken. Something interesting had come up? That usually meant he had a new assignment.

Even after all these years of being close to her father, Amy was still unsure about his work. She believed it was some sort of research for the Government but what it entailed exactly, she really had no idea. Occasionally it had meant trips abroad, but they had usually taken place in term-time when she'd been away at boarding school or, later on, at university. Surely he would never have gone away just when she was due home?

But clearly, he'd gone a little further than to the takeaway down the road. What to do?

'Dad's mobile,' she muttered.

She dialled the number and waited. There was no reply and she wandered towards her father's study. She could hear his mobile ringing and tracked it down to the desk drawer. The ringing stopped as she picked it up and in her ear, her own phone gave her the automated message: 'The person you are calling is not available. Please try again later.'

'Well, thank you very much. Why do you have to sound so delighted that no-one's answering?' She disconnected her own mobile and dropped her father's phone back into the drawer. He would never have gone far without it, surely?

★ ★ ★

She made some coffee and grimaced as she had to drink it black. Someone must know *something*. Uncle Henry. She rushed to the phone and dialled the number of her father's oldest friend.

'Uncle Henry. It's Amy.'

'Amy, my dear, how are you? Jeremy said you were coming home. He was so looking forward to seeing you.'

'That's just it. He told me he couldn't wait, but he isn't here. I suppose you've no idea where he could be?'

'What do you mean, he's not there?'

'Exactly that. I've just got home and the house is empty — all in darkness and no food in, nothing. There was a stack of mail on the floor so he must have been away for a day or two.'

'That's very odd. He never said anything to me. I mean to say, if he was planning a trip he would have told you, or if it was sudden, surely he'd have phoned me and asked me to meet you or something. Look, do you want me to come over?'

'Thank you, I'd like that. It feels a bit strange being here on my own — especially after being so excited. It's all fallen a bit flat.'

'Give me ten minutes. Put the kettle on, and we'll decide what to do.' He put the phone down and she sat back with a sigh.

Dear Uncle Henry. She'd known him all her life. His son Greg had been her playmate for many years, until they had grown apart during her boarding-school days. Once they'd both gone to university they had occasionally met up during the vacations for a drink, but no more. She had heard nothing of him since beginning her year in France, and she wondered what he was like now. Blue eyes, a wide grin, and a keen sense of fun was her fond memory.

She went into the kitchen and put the kettle on as instructed. Not that it would do much good, unless she could find some teabags. She looked in the cupboard and saw several tins of food, beans and such. That was something, even if there was no bread to make toast. Really, she needed to go and buy supplies or go hungry.

Before long, she heard a car stop and she rushed to the front door.

'Uncle Henry! Thank you so much for coming over. Sorry if I've spoilt your evening but I'm really grateful.'

'Well, look at you!' he said, drawing her into a big hug. 'What a gorgeous young lady you've turned into. I can't believe how much you've changed in only a year. Just wait till Greg sees you.

All his girlfriends will be kicked into touch right away. But I mustn't waste time — now, any clues as to where your father might be?'

'Nothing. Dad told me that something interesting had come up, but he said nothing more. It usually means some new assignment or other, but I can't believe he would go away and say nothing, nor that he'd forget to leave any message for me. His desk is the usual mess with nothing particularly special that I could pick up on. Loads of books piled up, several open at various pages. There's no food of any sort in the place, and the waste bin stinks. Whatever else, he usually empties that.'

'It's a bit like the Marie Celeste.'

'Except that there's no food left on the tables or anything. There are some letters — several days' worth — but I can't see any real clues.'

'Let's have a look.'

Amy picked up the collection of envelopes and handed them to Henry.

He flicked through them, hesitating at the lawyer's package.

'I wonder why he's been consulting Jekyll and Co?'

'I think they're his usual solicitors, but I've no idea why he might have anything from them.'

'This is his credit card statement. That might tell us something — something he's bought, perhaps?'

'*I* couldn't open it. He'd be furious. We have an unwritten code that we don't open each other's mail.'

'Fair enough, but we need something . . . *anything* to go on.'

'OK,' she agreed doubtfully. 'I hate doing it, though.'

She ripped open the envelope. There was nothing special. Supermarket bills from last month and a couple of mail order items, including the book.

'He hasn't booked any flights to exotic places or bought anything out of the ordinary,' she observed.

'Maybe the solicitor's letter might give a clue?'

'No — I really can't open that. It says private and confidential on the envelope — I must respect that.'

'But we have to do something. Will your scruples allow you to look at any of the other letters?'

'I don't know. Maybe. Oh, this is horrible!' Amy felt tears burning at the back of her eyes and she swallowed, hoping to stifle them.

'You have looked everywhere, haven't you?' Henry asked. 'I mean, you're sure he isn't upstairs or anything?'

'Lying in a heap somewhere? No, of course not. I'd have been in a real state, wouldn't I?'

'What about his car? Is that in the garage?'

'Oh — I haven't looked there.'

'OK, I'll go while you scan through some of those letters.'

Henry went through to the garage which opened from the back of the hall, and flicked on the light. The elderly Volvo was still in its place.

Amy ripped open the typewritten

envelopes but they were of no help: a letter from the water board warning of the supply being cut for work, and a request from a charity for a donation.

'The Volvo's still there, so at least you'll have transport. Anything in the mail?'

She shook her head, feeling the tears threatening again.

'Look, why don't you come home with me?' Henry offered. 'You can stay with us for a day or two until we can perhaps find something out. It's getting late now and there's nothing we can do till morning. I expect you haven't eaten either?'

'No. We were planning a celebration meal when I got back. A takeaway or something. But I couldn't impose on you. It's not fair on Auntie Pamela.'

'Nonsense. She'll be delighted to see you, and Greg's coming home in a couple of days, too. He'll want to catch up. It seems like the best solution to me. Now, if you're up to it, why don't you drive the Volvo over and then you'll be independent if you need to go anywhere tomorrow?'

'Thanks, Uncle Henry. I must admit, I don't much like the idea of staying here on my own. Not in the circumstances.'

'Jolly good. I'll give your Aunt Pamela a quick call to get her organised. Oh, and it's about time you stopped calling us Uncle and Auntie. Makes me feel old.'

'Thanks . . . Henry,' she whispered shyly and gave him a hug.

She picked up her smaller travel bag with all her toilet things and a change of clothes and took it out to the garage. Then, on impulse, she went back inside and collected the package from the lawyers. Maybe she *did* need to suppress her qualms and open it.

She started the car, pressed the control to open the automatic garage door and drove out. Henry was waiting at the entrance to the drive and she followed him to the warmth and safety of his home.

It was almost one o'clock before they finally got to bed. The story had to be repeated to Henry's wife, while Amy ate the simple meal Pamela had prepared for her. They opened a bottle of wine and gradually Amy relaxed. All attempts at making plans were left till the morning.

'I have a lecture at ten, but apart from that I can be free for most of the day,' Henry promised. 'We'll get in touch with your father's central office and see what they have to say. But tonight, try to get some sleep, and stay in bed as long as you like in the morning,' he instructed Amy.

Pamela fussed round her guest until she seemed a bit more settled. She was fond of her honorary niece and had always tried to mother Amy a little to make up to the girl in some small way for the loss of her own mother

'Thanks, Auntie Pam. It's very kind of you.'

'Nonsense, dear. And drop the 'Auntie', do! As Henry says, it makes us feel old. I'll give Greg a call in the morning, see if he can't come down a bit early. He'll be a help to you, I'm sure.'

Despite all her worries, Amy fell asleep quickly, and when she awoke in the morning she could hardly believe that she had slept through till almost ten. She had a shower and went downstairs to the smells of fresh coffee and grilling bacon.

'That smells wonderful. Thank you.'

'I heard you go into the shower, so I started cooking. I don't suppose you usually eat breakfast but I thought you might need it this morning. Oh, and I called Greg and he's able to come down this evening. He's working in Exeter now, so not too far away. He'll be with us for supper. Now, sit down and eat up.'

When she had eaten her fill, Amy began to feel more positive.

'I think I should start by calling

Dad's office. Or what he calls the office, though he works mostly at home. I picked up the number from his desk last night. They might help with something.'

'Go into Henry's study and use the phone there.'

'Thanks.'

Henry's study was the exact opposite of her father's. Everything was neat and rows of immaculate files lined the shelves. There was a framed photograph of Greg on the desk. She glanced at it, wondering if he'd changed much in the last year. She had always thought of him as almost a brother but how would they feel now they had both reached adulthood?

She sat at the desk and pulled the scrap of paper with her father's office number out of her pocket, then she drew the phone towards her, dialled, and waited.

When the call connected, she was asked a series of questions, which she assumed were a security route set up by her father: the name of the kitten she'd had as a child, and on which birthday she had been given her first bicycle. There were several questions to which only she would know the answer.

'This is all very James Bond,' she told the woman at the other end.

'We have to be certain you are who you say you are,' she was told crisply. 'Your father works on some sensitive information.'

'Oh, so you do believe Jeremy Poolley *is* my father then?'

'I am now satisfied of that fact. Now, how can I help?'

'My father seems to have gone away.'

'That's right.'

Amy's heart leapt with relief. Obviously he had been sent out at short notice and maybe had hoped to be back before she arrived.

'Thank goodness! Are you able to tell me where he's gone and for how long?'

'Well . . . ' The woman sounded doubtful. 'I assumed you would know. He's booked a month's leave to take a holiday with you. Walking or something? More than that, I can't help you, I'm afraid.'

'Oh, but . . . can I at least give you my mobile number? Will you please call if you hear anything?'

'Very well.'

Amy gave it to her.

'I'm afraid I can't help you any further,' the voice told her, and the connection was broken.

Amy sat staring at the machine. All this hush hush stuff was slightly alarming. She wanted to know more, but obviously that woman was never going to say anything else. All the same, she had detected a note of anxiety in the woman's voice, and the abrupt end to the conversation made her own fears rise again.

She went into the kitchen and gave the news to Pamela.

'I've learned nothing helpful. Maybe I should try calling the hospitals in the area? Dad might have had some sort of accident . . . lost his memory or something. It's possible — unlikely, but possible. Then I'll call the police. They can start a search. The car being in the garage makes an accident seem less than likely, though.'

'That all sounds sensible, dear. But why not wait till Henry gets back? Let him make the calls for you.'

'Thanks, but I'd rather get on with it. I can't stand this waiting and doing nothing. I'm fine, really. But maybe I should go home and use our phone. I may be on for some time.'

'Don't be ridiculous. I'd prefer you to stay here where I can keep an eye on you and make sure you eat properly. Now, have some coffee and we'll wait for Henry. He'll be back soon.'

She drank her coffee and went back to the study, where she worked her way through all the hospitals, including some of the tiny community hospitals in the area, but to no avail. Then she called the police.

They seemed a little dismissive at first but gradually began to take her seriously. They wanted to look round the house and see a photograph of the missing man. It sounded grim, 'missing man'. So impersonal — and like it had nothing at all to do with her dad.

Henry took her round to her home and accompanied the police as they inspected what seemed like every inch of the place.

'We'd like to take a look at his computer. Can you turn it on, please? There might be something there we can use.'

Amy hesitated.

'His work is very confidential. Government stuff. He had to sign the Official Secrets Act. So I'm not sure it's permissible for you to look at his work.' Amy was anxious. All she wanted was for them to put out notices to wherever they put them and see if anyone had seen her father.

'All the same,' said the constable, 'we have to take a look.'

Reluctantly she switched it on and they waited for it to boot up.

'We'll just take a look at recent emails for starters and see if we find anything there.'

There was virtually nothing since her own last message to him the previous Saturday. They had spoken on the phone on Sunday, and it was a fair assumption that he had left the house sometime on Monday. Four days ago. Since speaking to him, he had cleared out the fridge, maybe tidied the house a little, and then disappeared. But he had left the waste bin, as if he hadn't intended to be away for long.

She handed over one of her favourite photographs of him and watched as one of the policemen read through the opened letters. She so hated the intrusion into their affairs. She was glad she had left the legal document at Henry's house. At least they weren't going through more of their private business.

'OK, Miss. I reckon that's about all we need for now. Where are you staying, so we can contact you?'

'She'll be staying with me,' Henry broke in before Amy could answer. 'That is, with my wife and me for the next few days.'

'Very well, sir. Thank you. I have a note of your home phone number and Miss Poolley's mobile. We'll contact you as soon as there's anything to report. And you'll keep us informed if you hear anything from Mr Poolley? I expect it's just a trip away and he forgot to tell you.'

'Well, I doubt that. But thanks.' Amy was less than convinced that she would hear anything more from them.

She collected a few more clothes and did another check around the house, and then they drove off.

'I don't really know what to do. I can't bear just sitting around waiting for the phone to ring,' she told Henry. 'I'd go looking for him myself if I could even think of the first place to look. Are you sure he said nothing to you, Henry? Nothing about his work or any plans he might have?'

'Nothing more than I've told you already. He was looking forward to you coming home and maybe having a few days away somewhere with you. Oh, look — Greg's home. That's his new car. Pride and joy doesn't come close!'

The shiny black Jeep was parked outside the house, and Amy grinned.

'He always wanted one of those, didn't he? I can't wait to see him.'

'You don't have to.' Henry smiled as his son came rushing out of the house.

'Amy!' he yelled, pulling her into his arms and giving her a kiss on the cheek. 'It's so good to see you. See? I got my Jeep after all these years. Say, I'm really sorry to hear about your crisis. I came home as soon as I could get away. Well, look at you! Whatever else is going on, you look gorgeous.'

'Oh, Greg, it's so good to see you. And I'd say you've scrubbed up pretty well yourself. I've missed you.'

'Well, if you will go swanning off to far-flung places . . . '

'France is hardly the other end of the

26

world! But I've been working hard and I'm more than ready for a break. How about you? What are you doing with your life?' They walked into the house as they chatted, Greg's arm resting round her shoulders.

'I'm now a respectable computer technician. I use the term 'consultant' in my more extravagant moments. I love it. So, what's the plan now?'

'I'm supposed to sit back and wait for the police to come up with something. I'm not sure I can bear to do that,' she confided. 'I might try to organise some sort of search myself . . . if I can think where to start.'

'Tell you what, I'll come with you. I'm due some leave. I'll make a couple of calls and free myself up for a week or so. What do you think?'

'Thanks, Greg, you're amazing. Oh, it's so good to see you again. I'm feeling better already.'

★　★　★

Over dinner, they tried to form a plan of action. Greg and Amy would begin a thorough search of her father's study to look for any clues that may have been hidden away somewhere. At the most, Jeremy had been missing since Sunday evening. The earliest date on the mail had been Tuesday, which could mean he had been there to pick it up on Monday. They could look for any other discarded envelopes in the waste bins, to see if they could be more accurate about the time of his disappearance.

'None of us knows exactly what your father does, do we?' Greg asked. 'You were always very cagey about it.'

'I know it's some sort of research and that he signed the Official Secrets Act once. But I don't know how much research he could actually do from home. He went away occasionally, as you know. You know, thinking about it, he could have worked away from home a lot more than I ever realised. I was away at school for years and then university. And I mostly spoke to him on his mobile phone, or he rang me — so he could have been anywhere. I suppose he never said anything more to you, did he, Unc . . . erm, Henry?'

'Not really. We used to discuss various things but only in a superficial way. I must say, I was always very intrigued about his work. He's been at home more since the Internet came along.' Henry looked thoughtful. 'I always remember him using a computer, though — for many years before they became commonplace.'

'He did have a computer right from the start,' Amy remembered, 'and there was some sort of electronic mail connection, even in the early days — linked to some specialist university sites and used by the Government, too, I seem to remember.' Amy frowned, desperately trying to think of anything she had noticed in the past.

'I daresay I could access some of his things,' Greg mused. 'I'm pretty competent these days. But I don't want to get arrested for breaching national security or something.'

'I think we'll only do that as a last resort. We'll go over there tomorrow and see what we can uncover. Thanks — all of you,' Amy said, her voice warm with her heartfelt gratitude.

'Nonsense, dear. We're all family, aren't we?'

'Well, sort of. All the same, it's wonderful to have friends like you.'

They all tried to relax for the rest of the evening and to catch up with their news. She told them about her year in France and of her plans for the future. But always, the thought of her father crept into her mind and took over. Her deep-seated fear that something was seriously wrong just wouldn't go away.

At last it was bedtime and she could be quietly on her own. She was grateful for the company of this family, but she needed time to think and reflect.

'Night, Amy,' Greg said softly as they stood on the landing. 'It's so good to see you again. You've turned into quite a honey, you know.'

'Go on with you! It's me you're talking to, remember? Not some girl you're trying to chat up!'

'Yes, well . . . You've been away too long. I was forgetting. You're really just the kid with scraped knees and plasters stuck all over you.' He gave her a playful punch and she caught his hand, grinning as they always had.

'And you've turned into quite a hunk yourself, if I'm honest. You're not the kid with his pockets stuffed full of everything under the sun and then some more.'

He kissed her cheek as they parted and caught her hand for a moment. He seemed about to say more, but stopped himself.

''Night,' they said in unison and laughed again.

She shut her bedroom door, leaning against it with a smile, allowing the childhood memories to flood back.

But then she caught sight of the large envelope sent by the solicitors and was plunged back into the present.

Hesitantly she picked it up and turned it over once or twice in her hands. Then, suddenly, she made her decision and slit along the edge.

She stared at the documents. Two copies of her father's will. She felt tears burning and dropped the papers on to the bed. The covering letter asked him to read through it and they would arrange for an appointment to sign and witness the document. Nothing more than that. Nothing useful.

Why had he suddenly decided to make a new will? Surely his work couldn't be that dangerous? His life wasn't in danger, was it?

As her imagination worked overtime, she found tears rolling down her cheeks. Quietly, she lay down and pulled the covers up. She couldn't be without her father. She had no-one else. These were the last thoughts in her mind as she sobbed herself to sleep.

'It's Dad On The Phone!'

'It's no good,' Amy told Greg as she sat at her father's desk. 'I can't see anything of any relevance at all. There are random articles and pages of all sorts of stuff, none of which seems to connect with anything else. If I only understood just some of it, I might make the odd connection.'

'I can't find anything useful on his computer, either,' Greg admitted. 'I can't even tell if there's anything hidden anywhere. I should be able to, but either there's nothing to be found or your father is cleverer than most.'

She looked in the waste-paper basket but there was nothing. She pulled open his desk drawers and turned over the odd few papers. It seemed to be a random collection of old bills, scribbled lists and a lot of pens and pencils.

'Now I know why we can never find

anything to write with in this house — every implement's hidden in Dad's drawers!' She picked up a couple of pens and stuffed them in her bag. 'I might as well make use of them when I need them. Do you think I should phone the police and see if they've heard anything yet?'

'I wouldn't bother,' Greg said. 'They'll call you if they've any news.'

'I suppose so. Should I call his office again? They sounded a bit concerned when I spoke to them yesterday. They might have some new information.'

'Same thing applies — they'd call if they had any news. Look, how about we get a bite to eat at the pub? We can come back later and continue our search, though it's all looking a bit like a dead end.'

They drove to the local pub and sat at a small table in the corner. Amy didn't feel like eating much but Greg insisted and she ordered a ploughman's. There were a few other people in the bar but not enough to make the place noisy.

'Tell me about your work,' she said to Greg. 'So far all we've talked about is me.'

'Well, it's difficult to describe. Actually, it sounds pretty dull, but I love it. Sorting out computer problems. Trouble shooting. It's like tackling a complex puzzle and working through it to reach the answers.'

The food arrived and they ate while they talked.

'You always loved computer games, didn't you?'

'Yes. Well, I suppose I did. It gave me a feel for problem solving and I suppose I just built on that . . . ' He was interrupted by Amy's mobile phone ringing.

'Sorry,' she murmured. 'I'd better take this — it might be some news.' She pressed the button to connect the call and listened.

'Hello, Ames? I'm looking forward to seeing you, darling. It was a bumpy flight out here but I hope yours will be . . . ' Then it was cut off.

'Dad! Dad!' She almost screamed his name into the phone, but there was no answer.

'It was Dad!' she told Greg unnecessarily. 'I can't believe it!'

Greg leaned forward. 'What did he say?'

Amy was frowning. 'He called me 'Ames'. Said that he was looking forward to seeing me. That it had been a bumpy flight and he hoped mine would be . . . and then it was cut off.'

'He didn't say where he was?'

'No. I could hear something in the background though. A sort of humming noise. 'A bumpy flight out here.' He definitely said 'out here'.'

'Look at the number. It should be in the phone. What number was he calling from?'

She pressed the buttons until she found the record of the call.

'I don't recognise it. It's an international number — the plus sign then three four. Where's that?'

Greg grabbed the phone book from

the pay phone near the bar, and flicked through it to find the various dialling codes.

'Spain — it's Spain. Why don't you try calling back? You might just have been cut off accidentally.'

She dialled the number and waited.

'It's ringing.' It continued to ring for a very long time. 'Nobody's answering.'

'There's probably a fault on the line,' Greg tried to reassure her.

'Or he was prevented from speaking. And the phone was deliberately disconnected,' Amy suggested.

'Now you're letting your imagination run away with you! You're absolutely positive it was him? No doubt at all?'

'Of course not. I know my own father. But why would he be in Spain without his mobile — did I tell you I found that in his desk? And he called me 'Ames'. Why would he do that? He used to be furious if anyone called me that.'

'I remember. I used to call you that sometimes and he was so angry when

37

he heard me. I learned my lesson, I can tell you.'

Amy was frowning in concentration. 'Do you think he's in trouble — or was trying to warn me about something? Why else would he do it?'

Greg shrugged. 'I don't know. Let's go back to the house and see if we can find anything anywhere that has anything to do with Spain — phone numbers, addresses, anything.'

'The post's been,' Amy said as she pushed the front door open and met resistance. She picked up several envelopes and glanced at them. One was addressed to her.

She turned it over but recognised neither the postmark nor the handwriting. It was bulky and contained more than just paper.

'I wonder what this is?' she said, and was tearing it open before Greg could react.

'Hey, careful! It might be . . . OK. It's all right.'

She instantly picked up on his tone.

'Oh, goodness, you mean it might have been an explosive or something? Come on, Greg — don't let your imagination run away with you. All the same . . . ' she murmured as she pulled out the contents of the envelope. 'Goodness — someone's sent me a plane ticket. A flight to . . . to Spain! There's no clue as to who sent it but it's a London postmark. There's nothing else to identify it — no travel agent's name or anything. And there's a bus ticket and some euros . . . '

'When are you supposed to go?'

She scanned the details.

'It's for Monday morning — the day after tomorrow.'

'It's a good job I'm on holiday then, isn't it? I'll see about booking myself on to the same flight. Spain should be very pleasant at this time of year. Not too hot. Oh, I'm assuming there's no question that you're definitely going?'

'I suppose not. Not if Daddy is there somewhere. Where's Murcia?'

'I don't know. Somewhere down

south, I think. Where do we fly from?'

'Bristol. At least that saves the long drag to the London airports. But are you sure you want to do this? I don't know what I'm getting into and what I might be dragging you into.'

'My darling Amy, I wouldn't miss this for the world. And nor would I let you go on your own — especially if you think your father was trying to warn you off. It might be dangerous. Now, tell me, what else is in the envelope?'

'One hundred euros and a coach ticket — to Mojácar . . . whatever or wherever that is.'

'We'll look it up on the Internet. Anything else in the mail?'

'Just junk — it all looks pretty boring stuff. Hang on — look, the phone's flashing. There must be a message.' She pressed the message play key and listened.

'Miss Poolley? This is Unit One. We spoke yesterday. Would you give us a call, please? As soon as possible.'

'That's Dad's . . . well, his office, I suppose you'd call it. I wonder why they called here and not my mobile? I'd better call them back. They may have some news for me.'

★ ★ ★

She dialled the number and went through the same identification process as before. Greg smiled as he listened to her side of the conversation.

'Very James Bond,' he whispered and went back to looking at various piles of books.

'Hello. Yes, I got your message. What's going on? Have you found out where my father is?'

'Have you heard anything from him at all?' the woman countered.

'I had a very brief call from him, but it was cut off before he could say anything much. I looked at the number he was calling from, but there was no reply when I called back. It seemed to be in Spain, according to the dialling code. And then today, I was sent an air ticket to somewhere called . . . I don't

41

know how to pronounce it but it looks like Murcia and then a bus ticket to Mojácar. There are no clues as to who sent them except a London postmark.'

'Would you consider going there, Miss Poolley?'

'I am planning to go. If my father's in trouble and he needs me, I should go, don't you agree?'

'It has to be your decision. But I should warn you that there may be . . . implications. We can't take any responsibility for you, nor can we guarantee to get you out again if it should prove necessary. I'm afraid you'd be on your own. I should also say that we are rather concerned. We think he may not have travelled of his own volition.'

'Get me out? It's only Spain, for goodness sake! Europe, you know? You make it all sound rather . . . well, rather nasty. Dangerous even. Are you saying he might have been kidnapped or something?'

Greg looked up in alarm at that.

'I don't know what's going on but

you're not to commit to anything,' he muttered.

'We can do no more than speculate,' the voice on the phone said. 'It has to be your own decision. Keep in touch, won't you, Miss Poolley?'

'I'll have to use my mobile if I'm out of the country, and I don't want to go through this rigmarole each time. It costs a fortune!'

'I understand. Send a text message to two-zero-three-six-seven-nine-with just the word 'buzzard'. I will call you back immediately.'

'Buzzard?' Amy said incredulously. 'What's that supposed to mean?'

'Nothing significant at all. That's why I chose it. But I'll know it's you. Goodbye, and good luck.'

Amy hung up and stared at Greg.

'I've really no idea what's going on. It gets more mysterious by the minute. Code words. Mysterious letters. And why on earth was Dad making a new will?'

Greg stared and she remembered she

hadn't intended to mention the solicitor's package she had opened.

'You've lost me. Will? You mean he was worried about something and was making a new will?'

Amy nodded.

'With any significant changes?' he pressed.

'I've no idea. I never saw an earlier will. Look, I need to put a few things together for my trip.'

'We can do that tomorrow. I'd like to go home now and see about getting me a ticket, too. Because you're most certainly not going anywhere on your own.' His arm had found its way round her shoulders and she realised she rather liked it . . . But this was Greg. Her old 'mate' Greg.

'Well, thanks. I'd certainly be happier to have a big strapping bloke with me. The office or whatever it is were quite mysterious on the phone. Secret code words and comments about not being able to help me. 'Won't be able to get me out,' she said. What *is* going on?'

'Don't worry, love. I'm sure it's all just some misunderstanding. Perhaps your father booked you a lovely holiday and wanted it all to be a surprise for you.'

She looked at him hopefully.

'Do you really think so? But it's a weird thing for him to do, quite out of character. And why all the mystery?'

'Come on, let's make a move. We'll come back here tomorrow and pack what you need and see if there's anything new happening.'

★ ★ ★

Amy sat quietly through the short drive back to Greg's home, her mind dancing round the strange happenings of the past couple of days. Very little made sense. Why had her father — and she was certain it had been her father calling — why had he used a name for her that he hated? Was it some sort of warning? What was he involved in that made it necessary to use code words and go through all these checks just to speak to someone?

Pamela was waiting anxiously for them to return. Henry had retreated to his study and was busy preparing his next week's lectures but he came out to hear the news.

Once everything had been explained, Greg's parents were both adamant that he should accompany Amy. They didn't like the fact that she was making the trip in the first place but they could see that she was set on the idea.

'I don't think either of us is very happy about it, not one little bit, but at least if Greg is with you, you'll have someone to look after you,' Pamela said.

'And who's supposed to look after Greg?' Amy asked with a grin.

'Oh, we gave up on him years ago,' Henry replied. 'He's quite big enough to look after himself nowadays.'

'I'll see about booking my flight,' Greg said. 'I've got my laptop so if I can use the phone plug for a while, I'll get to it. Oh, give me that ticket, Amy — I need the flight number.'

'Are you sure you'll be all right, Amy dear?' asked Pamela. 'It must be such a worry for you. Well, for all of us. Your father's office couldn't help you in any way?'

Amy shook her head. 'Just the opposite, if I'm honest. They were hinting that he might have been . . . well, kidnapped, I suppose, though that sounds a bit melodramatic. I don't even know what work he's doing at the moment. He said it was something new and interesting, but you know my dad — always very cryptic about everything.'

'Good heavens, it just doesn't sound real. It's like it's one of those television dramas or something. You're sure it isn't just some sort of a surprise for you?'

'I really don't think so. It all sounds more sinister than that. I'm very worried and a bit scared, if I'm being honest. I'm so grateful to you all for helping me out. And I hope I'm not getting Greg into any sort of danger.'

'Oh, don't worry about him. He'll be fine. He's a careful sort of person these days, and I'd be happier knowing you're together. Hopefully you'll find out it's all something and nothing and you'll end up having a nice holiday out of it.'

'Maybe,' muttered Amy. 'Let's hope so. Have you got a map of Spain anywhere, so I can look up where we're going?'

It took a while before she found the places. Mojácar was some way along the coast from the airport, and she wondered why that particular airport had been chosen when there was another one which seemed much nearer. Perhaps there wasn't a convenient flight.

She went to see how Greg was getting on.

She found him concentrating hard at his computer, and she stood watching for a few minutes as he efficiently found what he sought. He frowned occasionally and she noticed the wrinkles in his forehead, so well remembered from their childhood. Whenever they'd played board games, he'd had the same expression.

She smiled fondly. Seeing him as an adult felt slightly odd. Greg had always been just a boy she knew, but the lifetime of years of closeness came back to her and she felt a deeper affection. And she acknowledged that it might be something more than a long-term, sisterly affection.

She gave a start as he leaned back and spoke.

'I've managed to get a seat but it's not exactly cheap, not this close to departure. Still, not to worry.'

'I'm sorry. I'm pretty broke myself. I haven't been earning anything worth speaking off for the last year, and with Dad — well, with the situation as it is, I haven't got access to any of his money.'

'Oh no, I wasn't expecting you to contribute! It was really just a comment about those so-called cheap flights we hear about. But there's no choice but to take it. I could come to the airport and try for a standby, but it might not work out and I'm certainly not letting you go off on your own. No way.'

'Well, thanks, Greg. I really appreciate your concern. I'll make it up to you one day, if it all gets sorted out.'

'*When*, not if,' he remarked. 'No worries though. Anyway, I'm earning a decent wage these days. OK, so now all we have to do is pack and decide on our plan of action. Do you speak any Spanish, by the way?'

'Not a word. Fluent in French but nothing in Spanish. You?'

'Nope. We'd better pick up a phrase book at the airport. Though they probably all speak English over there — it's tourist country, isn't it? Oh, and make sure you've got that cryptic office number in your mobile.'

'I've already put it in. I certainly mustn't forget that one! And I've stored the one that Dad used to call me, too, just in case. What on earth does it all mean, Greg?'

'I wish I knew. You've no idea what your father was working on? Not a hint?'

'No. He did once mention something to do with cell patterns and structures, whatever that means. And I know he spent days on end working on the computer. And, as I said, he did go away from time to time. Well, you probably remember — I came and stayed with you one time when he had to go away during the school holidays. I was furious that he wouldn't take me with him and you were mad that you had to play games with me instead of doing whatever it was you wanted to do. He went somewhere exciting and I was stuck here in Cornwall.'

Pam called them through for tea and they abandoned their speculations, agreeing not to say anything more in front of Greg's parents so that they wouldn't be alarmed.

Despite her concerns, Amy found

herself getting cautiously excited about the trip. She had never visited that part of Spain and in different circumstances it would have been fun looking up things to see and places to visit, especially with Greg in tow.

She gave a sudden shiver. If things turned really nasty for some reason, how would she cope? She was going into an unknown situation. The only saving grace was that Greg would be with her.

It seemed a long evening with everyone skirting round the main topic. Amy decided on an early night and planned to spend Sunday at her home, looking yet again to see if there were any clues she had missed. Then it would be a case of packing and an interminable wait until it was time to leave for the airport.

Her overactive mind prevented much sleep and she tried reading to while away the hours.

It was just before seven when a knock sounded on her bedroom door.

'You awake? Coming for a run with me?' Greg called softly.

'A run? Are you joking?'

'Not at all. A gentle jog will do you a power of good. Come on, it'll clear your mind.'

Amy lay back. The old Greg had been about as interested in keeping fit as she was in nuclear physics. Still, it might be nice to get some fresh air and exercise.

'OK,' she called. 'Give me five minutes.'

'You've got three and a half,' came back the reply.

She pulled on some loose trousers, a vest top and her normal trainers. She didn't have anything else suitable. She hoped he literally meant just a gentle jog; anything more would be a great strain on her unfit body.

They set off slowly along the road and turned towards the sea. Greg was clearly used to regular runs and he was almost running on the spot to allow her to keep up with him.

'Wow, how long have you been doing this?' she panted.

'I started it a couple of years back. I was spending too much time sitting at my computer all day. I was getting fat and lazy. I do three or four miles several times a week. I often jog to work, but that means following street routes which isn't so healthy with traffic fumes. But it's nice along the riverside.'

'I'm impressed. But I'm also worn out. I'm not used to this much activity. Can we stop now?'

Obligingly he came to a halt.

'You've done very well, considering. Walk if you prefer. Once we get back, take a shower to prevent stiffness and then I'm sure Mum will have one of her typical Sunday breakfasts ready.'

'And put back all we've just exercised off?'

'Muscle tone and fitness, that's what it's all about. Come on then — race you home!'

'No contest — I've had it! A gentle stroll is about all I can manage now.'

'At least I have some idea of your fitness levels if we need to run away from anything over the next few days,' he observed.

'You can always run for help. I'll have to stay put and talk my way out of anything! Not that I think we shall be in any situation. The more I think about it, the more I think your mum's probably right and it's just some sort of surprise trip. I bet Dad had to go away and organised it for me to join him.'

'Hmm. I can't believe there would be all this mystery surrounding it, though. And if that was the case, why didn't he speak to you properly when he called the other day? Anyway, we shall find out tomorrow. Spain . . . watch out, here we come!'

* * *

Amy insisted on spending the morning at her own home. She wanted time alone and besides, she felt that Henry and Pamela needed to see something of their only son.

The house was just as she had left it.

A faint musty smell was beginning to pervade and she flung open some windows. Then she unpacked her own suitcase that she had dumped in her room and stuffed a load of washing into the machine. She would need some clean clothes for her trip.

There were no further telephone messages and with a sigh she went back into her father's study.

She looked in the waste-paper basket again, in case she had missed something. She went into the bathroom and looked idly at the pile of magazines he always kept in there. Wait — was there something written there? She picked it up and stared. Hastily scrawled in faint Biro were the words: *Have to go away. Don't worry. Sudden trip. Stay till I get back. I'll explain then.*

Why on earth had it been written there? What exactly was he trying to tell her? To sit tight and stay here? No chance! Not to worry? Likewise — no chance! He must have gone to the loo before he left and that was the only place he could manage to leave a message. But why? Anyway, clearly he didn't want her to go after him, but she simply couldn't accept that.

'Oh Dad,' she murmured. She needed him. He was all she'd got.

Then she remembered the letters. Her mother's letters. She had found them one day several years ago when she was rummaging around in the loft. Her father had kept them hidden away, presumably because his loss had been too painful. Amy had read them all many times, without telling her father she had even discovered them.

She needed to read them again now. A contact with her family.

She rummaged around the desk and opened the drawer to find the key. It was an oldish looking key with a ring at the top and a curly design above the shaft.

As she tugged down the loft ladder, she heard the phone ringing in the hall but it had stopped by the time she rushed down the stairs. There was no message left. She dialled one four seven one to get a caller identity, but it was a number withheld. Disconsolately she went back upstairs.

She clambered up the ladder and switched the light on, by which she could see that there was very little stuff in there. Her father must have had a clear-out since she'd last been up there.

Half of the floor was boarded over. There was very little of interest apart from a few books, some boxes and a number of suitcases. Her father must have travelled light as his usual travel bag was still there.

She nearly jumped out of her skin as she caught a movement across the loft. Her heart pounding, she fingered her mobile phone in her pocket, ready to push the buttons if necessary to summon help. Trembling, she moved towards the spot and realised it was nothing more than a mirror. It had been her own reflection she had seen.

'Stupid mind playing tricks on itself,' she murmured.

She went towards it, treading carefully on the joists where the flooring had run out. Balancing carefully, she touched the wooden frame. It was a full-length mirror on a stand with drawers beneath the glass. She stooped to pull one open but it was empty. She fitted the key into the second drawer; a smooth click and it opened.

The package of papers, tied with a green ribbon, was still there.

With trembling fingers, she pulled it out. Balanced as she was, there was no way she could read it there, so she carried it back to where the main light was, near the trap door. She sat on the edge, her legs dangling down on to the ladder, and untied the ribbon.

There were several old letters in an unfamiliar hand and some photographs in a tattered folder, the sort photographic shops used to hand out.

She peered at the woman she had never really known. Her mother. Tears sprang to her eyes as she looked at the faded images, then she opened one of the letters, written by her mother when her father had been away at some time. She read the words, feeling slightly guilty. Voyeuristic even. If he'd wanted to share them with her, surely her father would have shown them to her?

She looked at another and tears did fall down her cheeks at this point. In a neat and precise hand she read the words:

I can't wait for our child to be born. Just another couple of months more. I pray you will hurry home and share this time with me. I long to see him or her and watch as our child grows up. We shall experience the joy of knowing we have created a very special human being from our own love.

She sobbed aloud. She knew that her mother had survived only a very few short weeks after the birth of her daughter. The fact that these letters and pictures were still locked away suggested that her father had never quite got over his loss.

There was a whole mountain of

emotions contained in the bundle and she realised she could not afford to spend time on it right now. Carefully she took them back to the mirror and its drawers and put them inside.

She heard the phone ringing again but she knew it would stop before she could possibly get to it. Maybe this time the caller would leave a message.

With a sigh, she left the precious bundle safely in its locked drawer. One day, she and her father might look at them together.

When she reached the phone, this time the light was flashing. She had received a message.

'Miss Poolley. I am sure you are there. I trust you will be joining your father tomorrow. I shall be waiting for you in Mojácar so do not let any of us down.' The voice was male and heavily accented. He pronounced Mojácar with a guttural sound in the middle.

What did it all mean? Who was she letting down, and precisely what was she getting herself and Greg into?

Amy was trying to digest this latest message when her mobile rang. She could tell from the caller display that it was Greg.

'Hi, Greg.'

'Everything all right? Have you made any new discoveries?'

'I found a brief message from Dad scrawled on a magazine beside the loo, suggesting I should sit tight. I don't know why it wasn't left somewhere more obvious for me to find. Maybe he had to find a way to leave it without anyone knowing. I suspect someone had come to collect him. Even his suitcase is still here.

'Oh, and I just got a strange message left on the answering machine from someone with a foreign accent, presumably Spanish, to say that he hopes I'm going to join my father tomorrow and that I'm not going to let them down.'

'Record the message on your mobile, would you? I'd like to hear it for myself. We might need to keep it and it might get wiped if you leave it on the phone.

I'd keep quiet about it to Mum, though. She'll be going into worry overdrive. Anyway, she says lunch is almost ready. We can go back afterwards if you need to do anything else.'

'I'll just put my washing in the tumble dryer and then I'll be with you. I'll have to come back later and pack. See you soon.'

She completed her chores, then recorded the mysterious message on to her mobile phone before she closed up the house.

★ ★ ★

'You both knew my mother, didn't you?' she asked suddenly, during lunch.

Pamela and Henry exchanged glances.

'Well, yes, of course,' Henry said slowly. 'But you've always known we did. What's made you ask out of the blue?'

'I was thinking about her when I was looking round the house. She did really want me, didn't she?'

'Oh, love, of course she did,' Pam said warmly. 'When Greg was born, she was just beginning her own pregnancy and she could hardly wait. She used to come round to our place and stare at Greg and touch her own stomach as if she could hardly believe it.'

'Maybe she really wanted a son.' Amy said in a small voice.

'Not at all. It was always a girl as far as she was concerned. None of us could believe it when she . . . when she died.' There was a hesitancy in Pam's voice as she said the words. It was clearly painful to her, too.

Amy pulled herself together.

'Thanks for the lunch, that was lovely. Can I help with the washing up? Then I should go and sort out my clothes and stuff for the trip.'

'You go and do whatever you have to — it won't take me long to clear this lot,' Pam assured her. 'Is Greg going back to the house with you?'

'Of course. She's had enough time to herself today. Anyway, I need to make sure she packs sensibly. You know what these women are like!'

'Well, I'll just go and collect my bag from my room,' Amy told them.

However, in her room she stood gazing out of the window and pondered the events for several minutes until Greg's impatient voice reached her.

'Are you ready yet? We have loads to do and time's whizzing by.'

Amy murmured some sort of response. Somehow she had to get on with the task in hand and deal with these emotional issues later — maybe after they returned from Spain.

She drew a deep breath and steadied her nerves.

'Just coming,' she called back.

Greg drove them round to her home in his Jeep.

'I've booked the car park at the airport, by the way. It's cheaper if you book it online. And I've booked my car in, so I can drive you.'

'You just want to show off to me, don't you?' she said as lightly as she could.

'Is there something wrong?' Greg asked.

'No, not really. Oh, well — my dad's gone missing, some mysterious Spaniard wants me to fly to a place in Spain that I don't know and have never heard of when all I wanted was a nice peaceful time while I sort out what I'm doing next with my life — but apart from that . . . '

Greg grimaced in sympathy.

'Sorry. I know. It's just that you seem distracted. More than before.'

'The pressure's getting to me the closer we get to flying out, I suppose.'

He stared at her and she knew he didn't believe her.

'Look, I know you're worried, but we must try to keep calm or Mum and Dad will insist on a police escort at the very least. Parents never stop being parents whatever age you are. Agreed?'

'Of course. We don't want them to be extra worried. So this is just a sort of holiday as far as they're concerned — right?'

Greg nodded. 'So, are you all packed and ready to go?' he asked brightly.

'Nah. I'll just fling a couple of tee-shirts and a change of undies into a bag. I can always buy something to wear if I need it. So why did you think I needed supervision with my packing?'

He grinned. 'I don't. But I'm saving you from my mother. She'll expect you to itemise each thing and have a debate about whether you have enough changes of suitable clothes for whatever event might happen. She'd have you taking nineteen options where one would do.

'It's actually pretty hot there at present — I looked up the weather maps — but take one warm thing in case it's chilly in the mountains, especially in the evenings.'

'My, you have gone all efficient in your old age,' she teased. 'Where's the old *Famous Five* attitude of waiting for an adventure to strike?'

'You know, I never did understand how those particular characters could always have such super exciting times and we just wandered around with nothing happening. Good old Enid Blyton.'

'Maybe we're making up for it now, only the clever scientist is my dad instead of Uncle Quentin.'

'And my mum's Aunt whatever-her-name-was, providing the huge meals all the time.'

'And lashings of ginger beer!' She smiled at him, but then her face became serious again. 'Thanks, Greg. For everything.' She touched his arm and felt his warmth.

'Hey, come on — you look much too serious to embrace this adventure in the right spirit. Whatever awaits us, we'll try to have some fun on the way. Like we used to?'

She smiled and nodded, hoping he was right. She had so many bad thoughts running through her mind. It had been the wrong time to discover the letters and photographs and to read her father's note.

At the house she pulled her things

out of the tumble dryer and carried them to her room to pack.

'Is that it?' Greg asked in surprise when she came down with her rucksack.

'You said we wouldn't need much,' she pointed out. 'I've got the essentials, and my toilet stuff is still at your place. I need to buy some more sun screen at the airport, that's all.'

'Oh, dear, Mum's never going to be happy with such a small bag! She'll expect to examine exactly what you're taking and add a whole load more — you know what mums are like.' He bit his lip. 'Sorry. That was tactless of me. I wasn't thinking.'

'It's OK. I'm used to it by now. Should be, shouldn't I? Come on — let's go. I need to check all the doors and windows, and then we'll be off.'

She glanced round the house, wondering if there were any more discoveries to be made. Well, they would have to wait now. She checked her bag one final time for passport and tickets, and then she was ready.

Flight To Spain

It seemed a long evening, with Amy's mind fully engaged on the things that were happening to her, while the others tried to make small talk and watch TV.

It was only nine-thirty when she finally decided she could take no more and excused herself.

'I think I'll have an early night — tomorrow could be a long day,' she said apologetically. 'We don't know how long everything is going to take and with possible flight delays and everything . . . '

'Of course. Go on — we really don't mind. I can see you're thinking of other things. I just hope you can get some sleep. I'll bring you some cocoa up in a few minutes,' Pamela promised.

'Thank you. Thank you all, for everything.' Pamela gave her a hug and patted her arm as she left the room.

Greg was right about his mother. She tutted over his bag and the contents, and offered Amy various bits and pieces of advice when she caught sight of her rucksack next morning.

'Is that all you're taking? Are you really certain you have everything you might need? Plenty of spare pants and socks? And something smart in case you get invited out to dinner somewhere posh? You might need extra socks if it's cold at night . . .'

'Leave her alone, Mum! She's been looking after herself for years.' Greg was grinning as he spoke and pulled a face at Amy as his mother confirmed his predictions.

'Do you think we should tell police that I shall be away for a bit?' Amy said.

'I think you should,' Greg agreed. 'Without telling them all the implications, of course. They'll always be able to call Mum and Dad if there's any news.'

So Amy called the police and

explained that she was going to Spain with a friend.

'They seem to think it's a bit odd, but I hinted that we have friends there who might know something,' she told Greg afterwards.

'Right. Well, we'll be on our way. We've both got our mobiles, Dad, so we can text you if there's any news. But don't worry if you don't hear for a while — we mightn't always be in range of a signal.'

'Oh, dear,' Pamela fretted. 'You will be careful, won't you? I'm really not sure you should be going like this.'

'Of course we'll be careful. We're all grown up now, Mum. Bye now.' He gave his parents a hug each, then loaded the bags into his precious Jeep.

'Henry, we shouldn't let them go,' Pamela said anxiously.

'It's all right, love. Like he says, they're adults now.' He tried to sound cheerful, but he, too, was very concerned about this trip.

Amy hugged them both and thanked

them again for their care and support. Then it was time to start their trip.

* * *

The road was busy and progress slow. Luckily they had allowed plenty of time, knowing well the notorious main route out of Cornwall. They decided to wait for something to eat until they reached the airport.

'I want to buy a few things in the shops there, too,' Greg told her.

'Such as?'

'Well, I thought we should get a torch and a map. Oh, and a phrase book. I wondered, too, about a compass. It might be useful if we get ourselves lost or something.'

'It all sounds very boy-scout and be prepared,' she teased.

When they reached the airport, the parking was easy and they quickly found their way to the check-in. They decided to put the luggage in the hold, despite it being small enough to carry on the plane with them.

'It saves having to lug it round the terminal while we're waiting,' Amy suggested.

They spent a long time in the travel shop, where Greg insisted on buying his compass and various other items, including a small pack containing a foil survival blanket.

'Why on earth? What are you expecting to happen on this trip?' she asked, beginning to feel exasperated.

'We might get stranded somewhere at night — you never know. We can huddle together under this and it could save our lives.'

'I think you're going a bit far. This is southern Spain, for goodness' sake, not some distant Arctic hideaway.'

'Well, it needn't concern you. It's only tiny and I'm paying for it and I'll carry it myself. Now, if you've finished complaining, shall we get something to eat?'

They were finally seated on their plane at one-thirty. Allowing for the time difference, they should be landing in Murcia at around four o'clock.

'We don't know how long it'll take to get to Mojácar,' Amy observed. 'I doubt it'll be before dark. If this man who was on the phone is meeting us there, we could be in for a late night. I don't much like the thought of not seeing where we're going, either, if we drive somewhere in the dark.' She was feeling quite nervous.

'He might get a bit of a shock to see me, too. Maybe he won't agree to take me along,' Greg commented.

'Don't say that! I'm not going anywhere without you. Besides, I might need to share your survival blanket,' she added with a grin.

'Don't joke about it. Just make sure you've got your mobile phone safe at all times. It might be as well to put it on silent so that if anyone calls it doesn't give it away.'

'I've got a security belt thing — I'll put my phone in there and I can tuck it right inside my trousers.'

'Yes, that's good.'

'You really do sound worried, as if there's something seriously wrong . . . '

'To be honest, I think there may be, and I don't want you in danger — well, no more danger than we can help.' He took her hand and held it tightly. 'You know, I never realised until now how precious you are to me. We've taken each other for granted most of our lives, haven't we?'

'I s'pose so,' she agreed, then frowned slightly. 'You're very sweet, but I'm not sure what you're trying to say. Anyway, this isn't the time to talk seriously about anything between us. We need to concentrate on what's going on. Maybe we should try to have a nap? I don't know about you but I didn't exactly sleep well last night.'

She leaned back and closed her eyes, but there was no way she could sleep. How mad was it to be travelling to an unknown country with tickets sent by an unknown man? But she needed to find her father. Besides, she had Greg beside her — he was surely a match for anyone.

'Set your watch forward an hour,' he instructed as they neared arrival. 'It's ten past five here.'

They watched the huge lagoon spread out beneath them as they flew along the coast. Tall white buildings shimmered some way out over the seaward side of the lagoon, looking for all the world like a mirage.

They landed with a bump and were welcomed to Spain in three different languages. The heat struck them as the door was opened.

'It's good that we have your blanket to keep us warm,' Amy teased as they made the long trek into the terminal.

They seemed to be waiting for ages for the bags to come off the plane but finally they were heading through Customs.

'Are you interested in seeing properties in the area?' asked a woman in a smart uniform as they emerged into the arrivals lounge.

'No, thanks,' they said in chorus.

'What about the chance to win one?'

'No, thank you,' Amy said irritably.

'I'll give it a go,' Greg said.

Amy shook her head and raised her eyes as she waited.

'What was all that about?' she asked when he had finished chatting to the sales rep.

'Now we have proof that we landed, if anything goes wrong. She'll be sure to remember me. I gave her my best chat-up lines!'

'You and a million others. But I get your point — a sort of informal registration of our being here.'

'Exactly. And who knows, I might win one of their charming apartments.'

'In your dreams! We'd better look for the bus stop and hope there is one.'

A woman watched them. Amy noticed her because she was holding a photograph in her hand and watching everyone who had come off the flight. But then she turned away and Amy thought no more about it. She had no idea that the woman discreetly followed them out of the terminal and dialled a number, watching as the pair boarded the bus together.

'Juan? She has arrived. But you have two subjects — repeat, two subjects. One male, one female. The target has a companion.'

* * *

It was just light enough to see the endless stretches of motorway, broken by strings of new building developments. Then there were high mountains in the distance, and wonderful coloured rocks showed up as the headlights caught them.

'It's a bit like those old cowboy films around here, isn't it?' Amy said.

'You're right,' Greg replied. 'I was looking stuff up about the area and they did film spaghetti westerns in this region. Cheaper than going all the way to America, I suppose. Can't see much of the place now. It's too dark. How are you feeling?'

'I'm not sure. A mixture of hoping to see Dad, and slightly fearful that I won't like what I find.'

'I know what you mean. I'm feeling a sense of anticipation and . . . well, responsibility for you. For us. It does feel a bit like some sort of spy thriller with us in the starring role. Unreal.'

'Hmm. Let's hope it is just some sort of elaborate surprise holiday. If I'm honest, though, I really doubt it.'

The bus journey lasted almost three hours, and when they eventually stopped in Mojácar, they looked around and wondered what to do next.

'Maybe we should book into a hotel?' Greg suggested. 'We'll see what we can find out in the morning, and at least we might have a decent night's sleep.'

'But our man said he'd be waiting for us. Well, me. Maybe he's not expecting there to be two of us, and he just hasn't recognised his passenger. I can't see anyone who looks as if he's meeting someone.'

They waited for a while, and then

walked along to what looked like the main road. There were several cafés and bars and food suddenly seem a high priority.

'I only have this hundred euros that was enclosed with the tickets. It won't go far,' Amy said in a worried voice.

'Don't worry — I'm loaded, baby,' he said in a dreadful American accent. 'Let's get a pizza. That'll stave off the hunger while we decide what to do next.'

They went into a crowded bar and ordered pizza and beers. There were quite a few young people there, and both English and Spanish were being spoken. Nobody seemed to have noticed them or was looking for them, so they relaxed a little and enjoyed their meal.

'I'll send my folks a text to let them know we've arrived.' Greg tapped away for a few moments and then turned to her. 'So, what do you think? Hotel for the night and start our enquiries in the morning?' he asked.

'I guess so. We don't have much

choice. There are loads of places over the road . . . but they look a bit expensive.'

'I said not to worry about bills. If you insist, you can sort it out sometime later when we're all safely back home. Personally, I'm pleased to share a bit of an adventure and have the chance to spend time with you. Once it's all sorted, we can enjoy a holiday.'

'I hope so,' Amy replied doubtfully. 'But you're right, it's good to be able to spend some time together.'

'We'll stick together like glue. You go nowhere alone, and only get involved in any conversations with strangers when I'm right beside you. Agreed?'

Amy nodded gratefully and gave his hand a squeeze. Greg made her feel much safer.

He paid the bill and they picked up their bags and left the bright lights behind them.

Across the road a very large hotel stretched for several blocks.

'Looks a bit grand for two folks with

back packs. Shouldn't we look for somewhere smaller?' Amy asked anxiously.

'It's getting late, and our money's as good as anyone's. Come on, it's here or nowhere.'

All the same, she looked around, wondering what could have happened to the man who was supposed to be meeting them at the bus stop. They had no clues at all about what lay ahead, or even why they were there.

The idea of a good night's sleep was fanciful in the extreme. They had adjoining rooms and Greg had warned her not to open her door to anyone but him. Amy tossed all night. She put the television on but it was of no comfort. She read and re-read the hotel brochure with all the facilities available and, at about three o'clock in the morning, wondered if Greg might like a swim. But she obeyed his instructions and stayed in her room, wishing it would get light and the day would begin.

It was around seven when there came

a knock at her door. She peered through the spy hole and to her relief saw Greg standing in the corridor.

'Morning,' she called brightly as she opened the door. 'I hope you got a bit more sleep than I did.'

'Not much,' he admitted. 'I watched some boring sport round-up on television but then I must have dozed a bit. You ready for breakfast?'

They went down to the dining-room where Greg was delighted to find a full English breakfast on the menu.

'Thank heavens!' he said. 'I was dreading a selection of sweet rolls and gooey jam. You should eat a proper breakfast, too. We don't know what lies ahead today.'

'We've been saying that for the last few days and eating big meals 'just in case'. I'll be putting on pounds at this rate.'

'Great, isn't it? Any excuse to eat! That's why I do my running.'

A waiter arrived at the table.

'Miss Poolley? There's a call for you.

You can take it in reception.'

'Wait for me,' Greg ordered. 'I'm coming too.'

'As you wish,' the polite young man said with a slight bow. 'Shall I keep your table for you?'

'Please. We've ordered already.'

'How did they know we were here?' Amy asked. 'Whoever *they* are.'

'Probably phoned every hotel in town till they got lucky.'

'Hello?' Amy said, picking up the phone at the reception desk. Greg was leaning close, trying to hear what was being said.

'Miss Poolley? Amy. You did not wait for me at the bus stop. I was not pleased. I shall await you outside your hotel in half an hour. That will give you time to finish your breakfast and check out. I shall be driving a silver four-wheel drive. A Freelander. I shall park in front of the hotel. Don't keep me waiting. We have a short drive into the mountains.'

'But where are we going? And where

is my father?' She got no reply as the caller had hung up.

She turned to Greg. 'He didn't mention you, so make sure you keep close in case he tries to separate us.'

'We know we're going into the mountains, at least.'

'I suspect there are mountains all around us, so that may not help much. Hey, I wonder if they can trace that call?' she suggested.

Greg nodded and asked the receptionist, but it was no good — the caller had withheld the number and they had no facilities for even a callback number.

They went back to eat their breakfast but neither of them could relax to enjoy it. Then it was back to their rooms to pack up and check out. Greg insisted on paying and she stood close to him, all the time looking out of the main doors.

'There he is — that Spanish looking guy with very dark hair.'

'He probably needs a four-wheel drive vehicle if he's driving in the mountains all the time. You've got your mobile switched to silent and well hidden?' he checked, and she nodded, patting her waistband. 'OK — here we go. Hang on tight.'

★ ★ ★

They emerged into the sunshine and approached the man.

'Miss Poolley? I am Juan. Welcome to Spain. I see you have a travelling companion. You wish that he accompanies you?'

'Yes, of course. Thank you.'

'We were not expecting a second guest but we have room available. Please, get into the car.'

They both scrambled into the back and Amy gripped Greg's hand. He gave her a squeeze and smiled cheerfully.

'So far so good,' he whispered, then turned his attention to the road, watching carefully to see the route they took.

'Here is Mojácar Pueblo,' their driver said, pointing to a collection of white buildings clustered right on top of the mountain. 'Old Mojácar, before the Playa was built and became such a tourist place.'

Greg tried to remember the names of various villages as they passed through and the numbers of the roads when he could see them. He planned to look at their map once they had stopped so that he knew exactly where they were.

They climbed through the rugged country, an arid area dotted with occasional palms and cactus. Greg noticed a village high above them, shining white in the sun. It was impossible to tell if they were old buildings or new ones. There was a sign at the edge of the village; *Las Minas*. Judging by the number of caves carved in the hillside around, they both guessed it was called The Mines.

They turned off the main track and went even higher. Amy gulped as they swung round tight bends with a great drop to one side and solid rock on the other. She prayed they didn't meet anyone coming down the mountainside. Juan made no concession to the narrow roads and barely slowed down as the next bend came at them.

'This is scary!' Amy whispered to Greg, her face white.

'Hang on, we must be near the top. Clearly he knows the road well. And we're travelling almost due north — I've been keeping our bearings.'

The driver peered at them through his rear-view mirror. 'You OK? We're nearly there. Your father is waiting for you.'

'I'm pleased to hear it. Actually, though, if you could slow down? I'm feeling a little sick. You know, the bends and everything.'

Juan laughed but slowed not at all, and Amy gripped Greg's hand even tighter. He put his arm round her and pulled him to her.

'You are a couple? Yes?' Juan asked.

'Yes, we're a couple.' Greg smiled at Amy.

She looked at him in surprise but

said nothing. It sounded rather nice, and it wouldn't do any harm if their hosts, or whatever they were, believed they were more than just travelling companions.

'It's strange that your father made no mention of a boyfriend,' Juan returned.

'It's all fairly new. I haven't seen my father for some time and he probably doesn't realise Greg and I got together.' Once the fib was started, it was easy to follow through.

They slowed down outside some gates. *Villa Parra-Moreno* was engraved on a piece of granite.

'Here is the villa.' Juan sounded the horn and the gates swung open.

Greg looked around to see how they were controlled, thinking it might be necessary to get out at some point. He was just about to give up when he noticed a camera mounted high on one of the posts. There must be a video link to the house, with the controls for the gates inside the house.

It was a long drive, lined with palms

and other exotic shrubs. The villa itself was low-built and single-storey, painted white and with a wide red pantile roof, typical of the area. A veranda ran round the outside, with graceful arches and offering plenty of shady places to sit out.

It was all very beautiful, but when they got out of the car, the view behind them was even more breathtaking. The Mediterranean sparkled in the distance, a blue shimmer of light with just a hint of haze hanging over it. They could see the Pueblo, a tiny speck of white to one side.

'What a glorious spot,' Amy said as she gazed around. There was a slight breeze, taking away the stifling heat of the town lower down. 'Are those olive trees?' she asked pointing down at long rows of trees, seemingly growing in bare earth and stones.

'Indeed. We grow our own olives and almonds, but it is too dry for much more. Perhaps you would like to come inside.'

'I can't wait to see my father. Is he here? Inside?'

'He is working at present, but you will see him later. I will get someone to bring in your bags. Come.'

They went into the large airy hall. White marble floors stretched endlessly, it seemed. It was cool after the hot sun and Amy shivered.

'I could do with your blanket after all,' she murmured.

'I told you it's cold in the mountains,' Greg returned. 'This is all a bit surreal, isn't it? I'm certainly not going to believe a word he says. And why is your father so busy working that he can't see us immediately? Just remember what I said — try not to get separated from me. I think you'd better be my new fiancée and can't bear to be parted from me.'

'That's fine by me. I'm scared, Greg.'

He held her close as Juan came indoors.

'I have sent your bags to your rooms. May I offer you some refreshments?

92

Coffee or cold drinks?'

'I'd love some coffee,' Amy said. 'But when can I see my father?'

'Later. He is engaged on important work at present.'

'But what's he doing here? Why is it necessary for him to be here and not working from his own home?'

'You have too many questions. I will arrange coffee and then you may go to your rooms.' He went out, looking irritated.

A maid in a black uniform brought in coffee and fruit. She said nothing as she put the tray on a small table, nodding at the pair and indicating that they should help themselves.

'It's all a bit grand, isn't it?' Amy whispered. 'But I feel as if we're being watched all the time.'

'It's quite possible. So maybe we'd better give them something to look at . . . ' To her surprise, he pulled her into his arms and kissed her soundly. 'Look as if you're enjoying it,' he said into her ear.

'I am, actually. It's just something of a surprise.'

He smiled again and as he held her for a moment longer, she felt her heart racing and wished his kiss was real and not pretend.

'I'd better pour the coffee,' she said softly.

They stood near the window as they sipped the strong coffee, getting their surroundings into some sort of perspective. They reckoned they were about twelve miles inland and, as far as they could tell, were in the only house on this particular road out of the village. It was probably getting on for two miles outside the actual village of Las Minas, Greg worked out. He would look it up on the map at the first opportunity.

'I could do with going to this room we're promised. I need the loo, for one thing,' Amy confided.

As if they had been heard — which they assumed they probably had — Juan came in to join them.

'Your rooms have been prepared. If

94

you will follow me . . . '

He led them along a cool marble floored corridor and opened a heavy panelled door. There was another corridor and a flight of steps going down.

'You are in the guest suite down here. Being high on the mountain means we need to dig down to build into the side of the rock. I trust you will be comfortable.' He turned and went back along the corridor, slamming the heavy door behind him.

'Do you get the feeling we've been locked in?' Amy muttered.

'Maybe. I'll go and check later. It looks like we have a room each, at least. With a shared bathroom. Saves any embarrassment.'

'Our bags are both in here. Which room do you want?'

'You choose.'

Amy opted for the one they were standing in before she went into the bathroom.

Greg examined his bag and knew

95

immediately that it had been searched. The map was gone, as were the compass and phrase book. His spare mobile phone had also been removed. It was an old one he'd packed in the bag, just so that anyone searching would find that and not be suspicious that they had travelled without one.

He tensed and looked around the room in case there was a surveillance camera or hidden microphone. He didn't want his search to appear obvious if, indeed, he was being watched.

He stood at the window and looked cautiously round the room. The light fitting looked the most likely place to put a camera, and he crossed the room slowly, watching to see if there was any sign of movement.

He caught a tiny flash as a reflection from the window caught the lens. So he was right. And if there was a camera, it would probably record sound as well.

His mouth set in a grim line. In many ways, he'd been treating this as a possible joke, a hoax even, but already it was proving to be something much more sinister.

Though he had to keep Amy alert to danger, he didn't want to scare her too much. He crossed to the bathroom and tapped on the door, and when she opened it, looking slightly puzzled, he went inside, shut the door behind him, and turned on the taps at full pressure.

'There's a surveillance camera hidden in the light fitting in my room,' he said close to her ear, 'so you can reckon on there being one in yours too. There's probably a microphone, too, so be careful of everything you say. My bag's been searched and they've taken the map, compass and my mobile. Oh, and the phrase book, too.'

She looked dismayed. 'Oh no! Lucky I've still got mine.'

'Don't worry, that phone was a plant, an old one I put in just in case. If they found one, they won't suspect I have another with me. We might need it,' he muttered.

'Oh, Greg, this is all getting very scary! Why on earth should they want to spy on us?'

'I have the feeling that we're here to blackmail your father into working for them.'

'But what's behind all this? And who owns this place? What on earth is going on?'

'Dad! At Last!'

Amy went to unpack her bag and, just as Greg had discovered, found that it, too, had been searched. There seemed to be nothing missing, however. Greg came back into her room and she pointed at the bag and nodded. His eyes gave a warning.

'Shall we go and take a look around outside?' he suggested for the benefit of anyone who might be listening.

'Great idea. I could do with topping up my tan. Poor Dad, having to work so hard in this glorious weather. I can't wait to see him.'

They went up the stairs and along the corridor to the door. As they had suspected, it was locked.

'Now what?' she exclaimed.

'We'll have to climb out of the window on to the balcony,' Greg muttered. 'We can always plead innocence and suggest that the door must have been locked by mistake. I'd like to take a look around.'

Back in Amy's room, they opened the window as wide as it would go, but it was too small a gap to climb through. It was the same in Greg's room. The window opened only a short way.

'This is ridiculous!' Amy exclaimed indignantly. 'We're trapped in here. I hope someone comes to let us out soon. I was hoping for some lunch before too long. It seems a bit odd to invite someone to stay and then to lock them in their room. Don't you agree?'

Greg almost laughed out loud. If someone was indeed listening, Amy was managing to sound most convincing.

'I must tell my father that I don't think much of his friends if this is the way they treat their guests,' she added.

'And we have such exciting news for your father. You don't think he'll mind, do you, darling?' He winked and, grasping her left hand, gently kissed her bare ring finger and looked up at her. Her heart gave an unexpected leap.

'About us being engaged? He'll be delighted. And I'm so glad you agree with me about having separate rooms until we're married.'

'Good girl,' he muttered. That would explain a lot to the listeners.

'What are we going to do?' Amy asked after a while.

'Hope that someone realises the mistake and comes to let us out before too long,' Greg suggested.

'We haven't even got a book to look at. What happened to the guide books and the phrase book? And the map? I could have sworn we put them in your bag. They're certainly not in mine,' she exclaimed, all innocence.

'Maybe I left them at the hotel. And I must have lost my mobile phone at the same time. That seems to be missing, too. You know, it's almost as if someone has taken them away — the very things that might help us know where we are. We can't even phone someone upstairs to let them know our problems.'

They sat on the bed and were quiet for a while, but nobody took the hint and came to let them out.

As time went on, Amy lay back and closed her eyes. After her sleepless night, she soon drifted off into a deep sleep, troubled by strange dreams. Greg slipped his arm round her, smiling fondly at her peaceful face. He leaned back against the headboard, holding her against his chest, and closed his eyes. It was hot and stuffy in the room and he quickly fell asleep too.

They were awakened by a loud bang as the big door was opened and shut itself again. They sat up with a start, unsure of where they were. Footsteps sounded on the stairs and they both ran to the bedroom door. It was the same maid who had served coffee; now she was carrying a large tray with a selection of cooked meats and salads, some fruit and two bottles of beer. Without a word she plonked the tray down on a table and went out of the room again.

'Excuse me!' Amy almost shouted. 'Just what do you think you're doing keeping us locked in here?'

The woman ignored her and went back up the stairs. They heard the door being shut again and a bolt being drawn across.

Greg grinned. 'At least you got your lunch. Two-thirty — about right for Spain, I suppose.'

She picked at the food, upset and angry about being imprisoned like this.

'Come on,' Greg cajoled. 'You must keep your strength up. We might not get fed again today.'

'Why are they doing this?' she protested. 'Why can't I see my father? We came over just as they told us to, but why? What for?'

Greg didn't like to tell her his own thoughts on the matter. Maybe Jeremy was being asked to do something he didn't like, and the fact that his daughter was now at their mercy could swing it for them. He would be forced to work.

Whatever the story, it was most unpleasant.

He stood looking through the window. There was a balcony of sorts running round the side of the house. Looking upwards, he could see a long stretch of wall which he assumed led to the upper floor. There was no way up there, even if he could have got through the window. Below them, the ground fell away steeply down the mountainside, presumably on the other side of the house from the entrance, as there was no sea view. In fact, there was not much of a view at all as the next mountain rose up just across a small valley. He couldn't tell where the boundaries of the house lay.

'There's a cave over there,' he said, pointing. 'I expect the mining went on all over this area. The whole place is riddled with caves and holes in the rock face. I wonder if they find anything nowadays?'

'I wonder if they use the caves for storage? It must be relatively cool inside. Save on fridge space. Oh, I'm so bored!' she complained. 'I was expecting to be doing something, not sitting locked away in some basement.'

'I thought it might have been a mistake until the food arrived and then we were obviously locked in again. It's like a prison! It's a shame I didn't bring my laptop, then I could have done some work, at least. Not that I'd have been allowed to keep it, I suppose.'

'You mean you think someone might have taken it? You mean you think someone took your mobile and the other things?' The heavy sarcasm in her voice nearly gave away the fact that she knew they were being watched, but Greg gave her a warning grin and raised his eyes towards the light fitting, reminding her that it wasn't safe to speak openly.

'I might have a shower. Do you want to scrub my back?'

'If you like.' She understood his hidden message. It was safe to talk when the water was running to mask their words.

He went into the bathroom and ran the water. She followed and they spoke in whispers.

'I'd better actually have a shower or they'll guess our tactics . . . I think I'll wait by the door on the stairs until someone comes down again. I think they'll bring us some more food, or at least collect the tray at some point. I could rush out and make sure the door stays unbolted for you to get out. I'll stuff the pillow into the bed and make it look like it's me, asleep.'

'But how can you do that if the camera's watching your every move?'

'Make the room dark — pull down the blinds. I'll pretend I feel unwell and go to bed early. You'll be all right, won't you?'

'Of course. We can't just stay here like this. I could try demanding to see my father, if anyone other than the silent maid appears.'

'We'll follow my plan, and you can try yours as well when someone comes. Say I've gone to bed and you're fed up.'

'No lies there then — I *am* fed up. Now, are you going to have this shower? You'd better be quick. We've been here for ages already. I'll turn my back.'

'And you'll scrub mine, I trust? As promised,' he teased.

'Get away! I'm leaving you in about thirty seconds, so get on with it.'

He flung off his clothes and drenched himself, then turned off the water and began to dry himself.

Amy left him to dress and slumped back on to the bed, and when he came out of the bathroom he told her he 'felt unwell' and was going to lie down.

'I've got a headache so I'll close the blinds and try to sleep. You'll be all right, won't you?'

'Of course I will. I hope you feel better soon.'

He kissed her as he left, and she lay back again, realising she quite liked her new role as Greg's 'fiancée'.

There was silence, not a sound except for the chirping of the cicadas and other night creatures outside the window. It was warm but a faint breeze took away the stuffiness she might have felt. She glanced at her watch. Six o'clock. It seemed like the longest day of her life. Perhaps she, too, would take a shower, if only to while away some time.

There was shampoo and soap provided and she lathered up liberally then stood still, letting the warm water stream over her body. However, the supply suddenly ended, and no matter what she tried it wouldn't start again. She'd heard tales of holidaymakers having to endure long periods of water cuts. Maybe it had been caused by them wasting water when they'd wanted to talk without being overheard. Wiping away the suds as best she could, she dried herself and went back to lie on the bed.

Presently she heard the door opening and footsteps coming down the stairs. She held her breath, waiting to hear if Greg would make it successfully.

There was a knock at her door and it

opened. It was Juan.

'Where is your companion?'

'He's lying down. He has a headache.'

'Very well. Come with me. I am to
take you to your father.'

Amy leapt up in excitement. 'At last!
Great! I can't wait to see him!' She
picked up her bag but Juan took it from
her.

'You won't be needing that. Leave it
here.'

She shrugged and followed him out
of the room, forgetting Greg's warning
not to go anywhere without him.

'I will look in on your companion,'
Juan said, and Amy froze as he opened
Greg's door. It was quite dark in his
room and the lump on the bed was
convincing. She hoped he'd managed to
slip out into the house while the door
was unbolted.

'OK. He's asleep. Come now. Follow
me.' Juan went up the stairs, pushed the
big door open and bolted it carefully
behind them both. If Greg hadn't got

out, he was again trapped down there.

Juan spoke again. 'So, you are engaged in marriage to this man?'

'Yes.'

'But you do not wear a ring and your father knows nothing of this arrangement. And you do not share your bed with him?'

'It's all very recent. And — not that it's any concern of yours — we decided to wait until we're married before we share a bed, as you put it. I was planning to tell my father when I saw him but he was away when I returned home.'

'I see. Come along. He is waiting for you.'

★　★　★

They went outside into the garden. Dusk was already beginning to fall and the sounds of night creatures filled the air. There was a heavy perfume from the flowers and the sharp scent of wild herbs everywhere. She could hear a fountain trickling somewhere nearby.

In other circumstances, Amy would have appreciated the beautiful night and the lovely setting, but her fears were taking over her mind. There was something decidedly sinister about this man and she was being led into a situation she couldn't control.

There was a building set into the side of the rocky cliff and they were walking towards it. Juan produced a key and unlocked the door. That made it obvious that her father was not here voluntarily. If he was, why was he also locked in?

Light streamed out of a well-lit room. There was a bed in one corner and an armchair. One wall was covered in book-cases filled with books that looked like those in her father's own study at home. There was an electric kettle and a jar of instant coffee. He wouldn't like that, she thought. He loved his strong filter coffee, insisting he couldn't function without it.

She saw another door to one side,

which Juan indicated she should enter.

She looked around her and then pushed it open. This room was just as bright and appeared to be a work room with a collection of bottles and tubes that looked like some sophisticated chemistry set. Sitting at a bench was her father.

'Dad!' she called out, running to him.

'Amy? Amy? Is it really you?'

'Of course it is,' she said, rushing into his arms. She hugged him close but felt his resistance.

'Oh, Amy, love.' He stroked her hair as he held her. His voice sounded strange, tense. 'It's good to see you but I'd hoped I'd put you . . . '

'That's enough. You see? I told you your daughter was arriving. Now she has. You have five minutes.'

'Five minutes? Dad? What's going on?'

'I'm doing some research here. Working for Señor Parra-Moreno — Ignacio Parra-Moreno. He owns this house and — well, he wanted to know more about some of the things I have been working on. But how are you? Oh, it's good to see you, even if I had hoped you wouldn't come.'

'It's all right. Greg came with me. He's lying down with a bad headache.'

'Ah, headaches. They're very common here. I suspect it's something to do with the water. I suffer very much myself.' He was staring into her eyes as he spoke as if he was trying to give her some sort of warning. Pulling her into his arms again, he indicated that there was something above them. Another camera, no doubt, she thought. He was warning her not to say anything as they were being monitored.

'I gather you and Greg have finally become engaged?'

'Yes,' she said hesitantly. 'But how did you know?'

'I was told, when I was informed of your arrival. They weren't expecting you to have a companion with you. This is something of a surprise to me, too, I must admit.'

'You know we've been friends for ever. I guess it was the logical outcome.'

The conversation was stilted with neither of them able to ask what they really wanted to know.

Her father did not look well. There were new lines around his eyes, clearly showing the stress he was under. It was becoming obvious that she really was here only to ensure his full co-operation with whatever work he was undertaking. His attempt at a phone message had been designed to keep her away, but in her own impulsive way, she had taken little notice of him, or simply not understood the implications.

She tried to speak cheerfully. 'So, you mentioned some new project last week on the phone. I take it this is what's keeping you here now?'

'Exactly that.'

'That's it,' Juan interrupted. 'You can see your father again tomorrow.'

'But we've hardly had time to say anything,' Amy protested. 'We haven't seen each other for ages and have heaps to catch up on.'

'Providing your father can achieve his target for tomorrow, you may see him again then. Perhaps for a little longer.'

'Come on,' Jeremy protested. 'I've been working as fast as possible. You can't rush these things. Everything is taking time to develop and mature. Rush it and the results will not be accurate.'

'Quiet! Get back to your work.'

'Come on, Amy, dear, let your father earn his keep.' Jeremy looked as if he was going to say something else but then clearly thought better of it.

'Do you think I could have something to read at least?' Amy put in. 'I shall go mad with boredom if I just have to sit around for another day.'

'I'm sure you and the handsome fiancé can find plenty to occupy yourselves.' Juan gave a nasty snigger.

'Not with you watching our every move!' she snapped back.

'How do you . . . What makes you think that?'

'I sense it's the sort of thing you would do,' she countered. 'So, do we get some reading material?' She glanced at the well-stocked shelves in her father's room.

'I doubt you would understand a word of any of it.'

'I can suggest something she might like,' Jeremy offered. 'My daughter is intelligent, as is Greg.'

'All right, but make it quick.'

Jeremy looked along the shelves and selected a couple of volumes. Juan took them from him and flicked through the pages, shaking them to be sure there were no loose pages or messages. Finally he handed them over with a nod of agreement.

'Thanks, Dad. Hopefully I'll see you tomorrow.' She kissed him and gave him a hug. 'Don't worry about us,' she whispered in his ear. 'We'll get you out.'

'Regards to Greg,' he added as she was almost pushed out of the door.

It was locked again behind her and Juan dropped the key into his pocket.

Amy had no choice but to march back to her own prison.

She felt tears burning her eyes. It wasn't fair. She needed to be with her father. What was he being forced to do? He rarely worked in a laboratory as such, not these days.

Her mind raced over the possibilities. Was he making some deadly weapon? A biological killer? She didn't even know if he had any expertise in that sort of chemistry or biology. But clearly there was a whole side of her father she did not know. She had seen no sign of a computer in his prison — presumably because he would have contact with the outside world if that were the case.

She remembered her mobile, tucked into its belt and hidden inside her trousers. Luckily they hadn't searched her. But why hadn't she thought of it before? Once she was back in her room, maybe she could find a way to text her father's office. It would be tricky with the surveillance camera watching her every move, but there must be some way she could do it.

* ★ ★

They arrived back at the main house and she was marched down the stairs again and sent into her room. Juan went to look again at Greg and seemed satisfied that he was still asleep.

Once he had gone, Amy looked at the two books her father had given her and frowned. Why had he chosen an obscure travel book about South American Indians and some biology book that meant nothing to her? Maybe it was just a random choice but it seemed strange. He knew she was hopeless at science subjects but maybe the South American book would be vaguely interesting, at least.

She glanced round the room. The lunch tray had been cleared in her absence but nothing else seemed to have been tampered with. She wondered if they were to be given anything else to eat.

She went to Greg's room, tapping gently on the door as she went into the dark.

'How are you feeling now?' she asked, trying to keep up the pretence. She sat down on the bed and touched the rolled-up pillow, pretending to stroke his forehead, then she leaned down, as if kissing his cheek, and murmured something about hoping he felt better in the morning.

'Night. You sure you don't want any food if they bring any?'

She even made a sort of deep grunt, hoping the watchers would think he was replying.

As she went back into her own room, Amy's heart was thumping. There was no sign of Greg anywhere. Had he managed to escape? Was he safe? Would he be able to get her out? The questions raced through her head.

With this wretched surveillance camera, she daren't try anything, least of all phoning anyone. She had also decided to switch off her phone altogether, as she had no means of recharging it. Though she had brought the charger with her, there were no sockets she could use.

She looked at the window. Swarms of insects crowded against the glass, attracted by the light. She switched it off and opened the window slightly. The cooler air was welcome and she stood looking along the valley below.

'You OK?' came a soft murmur.

'Greg!' she replied in a whisper. 'Where are you?'

'Balcony to your left. I could do with that blanket thing — it's got really chilly out here.'

'I saw Dad,' she told him. 'He looks unwell and very strained. I think he's being forced to work on something. He has a sort of laboratory, but I don't understand it — he isn't a biological scientist, yet that's what he seems to be working on.'

'I'm going to try to get you out later, when everyone's gone to bed. Have they given you any more food? I'm starving.'

'No, nothing. Wait, I can hear something now — I'd better go. I'll shut the window or the room will fill up with insects.'

She pushed it to and had just put the light on again and sat on the bed as the door opened. It was the maid again with a tray. She looked round suspiciously and burbled a load of Spanish that meant nothing to Amy before going out again and slamming the door behind her. Amy hoped she hadn't been questioning her about leaning out of the window, but if that was it, the woman had left without getting an answer.

The tray contained a dish with some sort of meat in it and some vegetables. There was a small salad in another dish and a couple of pieces of bread. There was also a carafe of red wine. For the benefit of the camera, she pretended to eat and poured some wine into the glass, sniffing it experimentally. It smelt slightly odd. Cautiously she dipped her tongue into the glass. It was either badly corked or something had been put into it. Maybe something to make her sleep? But how could she get some of the food to Greg? He was starving, he claimed.

She sat so that all the camera could see was her back as she pretended to eat her food. She did eat the salad and one piece of bread, and tipped up the wine glass as if she was drinking it. Hopefully, once the light was out, they wouldn't notice when she threw it down the sink.

After what she felt was a reasonable time, she set the tray aside with a napkin over it to hide the fact that little of the food and wine had been consumed and went into the bathroom to brush her teeth. Then she put out the light and sat on the bed. If the camera could still film in the dark, her plans were scuppered.

But then she had an idea. She picked up the blanket from the bed and hung it carefully over the light fitting, hoping the camera was completely hidden.

With luck, the sound would also be muffled, and her activities would be less noticeable. Hopefully, nobody would come to collect the tray till morning. Just to be extra safe, she jammed her rucksack against the door, trapping one of the fasteners so that the door wouldn't open.

She crossed to the window and opened it as far as it allowed her.

'Greg? Are you still there?'

'Of course. I gather you got some food.'

'Yes. They didn't bring anything for you but I saved you some of mine. It'll be a bit cold now but at least it's something. How can I get it to you?'

'There's a ledge outside your window. I'll walk along it — maybe I can stand and eat it there, or carry it back.'

It all sounded very impractical, but a starving man will doubtless risk anything, she thought.

She heard a scrabbling sound and soon she could make out a dark shape just below her.

'I've covered the camera and microphone but best keep your voice down anyhow. Here — there's a dish with meat and I've put the veg into it. Can you manage?'

'Great. I don't function when I'm starving.'

'I suspect the wine was drugged so I'm going to tip it away. They probably expect me to sleep very soundly.'

She could hear Greg eating the food quickly. She wasn't sure how he was managing to balance, or even how wide the ledge was.

At last he spoke again. 'Can you take the dish back? Thanks, that was great. I hope you're not too hungry — you seemed to give me most of it. So, how do you think your dad seemed?'

'Tense, and probably not best pleased to see me. We couldn't talk much as Juan was watching like a hawk. Have you managed to find out anything?'

'Not a lot. There are cameras everywhere. This side of the house is pretty steep so there doesn't seem to be much in the way of lights or anything. There are spotlights that come on with movement sensors on one side of the building — luckily the birds and large moths are taking the blame for most of that. Trouble is, I don't know where they are or who is watching. The whole place is done up like Fort Knox. What on earth have they got to hide?'

'What do we do next?'

'I need to try to get round to where your father is being held. Do you think he sleeps in there?'

'I think so. There's a bed in his room. Locks on the door and cameras and everything. Take care, Greg. If you get caught, they might . . . well, who knows how desperate they are? You don't think you should come back in? They'll discover you're missing in the morning.'

'I suppose if I could get out once, I could do it again. OK, you're right. I'll sneak back and just leave the bolt undone.'

'The maid will get blamed for leaving it undone. Serve her right, sour old puss that she is. See you soon.'

Gently Amy shut the window and dragged her rucksack away from the door, then she groped her way to the bathroom and tipped away the wine.

Eventually she heard the door creak open up the stairs and Greg's soft footfall as he came down. She whisked down the blanket from the light fitting and put the light on.

'Greg?' she called out. 'Are you feeling better?'

'Much better thanks. What's the time? I must have been out of it for hours.'

'I'm so relieved,' she said honestly. She gave him a huge hug and held him tightly, not wanting to let him go.

'Drugged wine,' he breathed into her ear. She gave a start, having quite forgotten that she was supposed to be asleep in a drugged state. She slumped against him.

'Sorry, love, but I just can't keep my eyes open a minute longer,' she murmured loudly.

He helped her on to the bed and covered her with the blanket, then switched off the light and went into his own room.

'End of day two of the big adventure,' he muttered.

Meeting The Señor

For whatever reason, they both slept soundly. When Amy awoke, the sunlight was streaming into her room. She looked at her watch and saw it was already past eight. She had slept in her clothes and felt itchy and grubby, and hoped the shower would be fully operational today.

It was, and after a swift refreshing shower, she put on clean clothes, then tapped on Greg's door.

'You awake?' she called softly.

'Yes. Slept like a log.'

'And feeling better?'

'Yes, thank goodness. I can't think what brought on that attack yesterday. I do get headaches from time to time but that was a blinder.'

'Maybe we'll get some fresh air today. That'll help. They can't expect us to sit in this room all day. Maybe we can read the books Dad gave me.'

'Books?' Greg asked innocently, raising one eyebrow. Amy gave a start. Of course — Greg was supposed to have been asleep all the time.

'Once you've showered, I'll show you. I saw Dad briefly last night, while you were out of it. I'll tell you all about it. I wonder if we'll get some breakfast? You must be starving after missing dinner last night.'

They heard raised voices from outside the door. A torrent of angry Spanish poured out. The pair looked at each other and suppressed a grin. Clearly, the unbolted door had been discovered.

An angry Juan came into the room. 'You are recovered?' he demanded.

'I feel much better, thanks,' Greg mumbled.

'And you have been in bed all night?'

'Of course. Where else would I be? You locked us in, remember?'

A smirk flicked across the Spaniard's face. 'Lucky for me, eh? Lucky you didn't realise the door had been left open.'

'Really? Like I say, I was out of it yesterday, and Amy says she slept very heavily, too.'

'That is good. The maid will bring you breakfast.'

'And what is our itinerary for the day?' Greg asked.

'There is no itinerary. You will stay here. It helps Amy's father to know she is here. He can be more productive in his work, knowing she is close by. As for you — ' he shrugged ' — it was your choice to accompany her. I can arrange for you to fly home today, if you like.'

'It's OK. We want to be together. But we need some fresh air and exercise. Maybe we could go outside — have a swim, maybe?'

'How do you know there is a pool?' Juan asked suspiciously.

'Every self-respecting Spanish villa has a pool,' Greg responded simply.

Juan seemed satisfied with the reply, though Greg realised he would have to be more careful if he wasn't to give away his tour of inspection the previous night.

Juan turned and went up the stairs noisily, and a few moments later, they heard someone else coming down. The maid. She gave them a cautious grin and set the large tray down, muttering something that they took to be an invitation to eat, then left them to it.

There was a large pot of coffee, a basket of rolls and some jam in a dish. There were also a couple of bananas and some grapes. Greg wrinkled his nose in distaste.

'The sort of breakfast I most hate. And not enough for a man who missed dinner,' he winked.

'You'll survive. I'm pretty hungry myself,' Amy told him pointedly, and he looked apologetic as he realised he had eaten most of her own dinner last night.

Amy poured the coffee and warmed her hands around the cup.

'I think Dad must be on the other side of the garden. It seemed quite a long walk last night and I didn't go through much of the house at all.'

'It certainly seems quite a place,' Greg agreed. 'Must have a lot of rooms upstairs.'

'I wonder how they generate their power? Getting electricity this far up the mountain must have been quite a challenge.'

'They'll have a generator somewhere. I bet the supply isn't all that reliable anywhere around here. I bet there's air conditioning in the main rooms, too. That uses up power like you wouldn't believe.'

After they had eaten everything and drunk all the coffee, Greg went off for a shower and Amy picked up the books her father had given her.

She flicked through the biology book, but it was rather advanced and would mean considerable study before she could understand any of it.

The other one, about South American Indians, seemed slightly more interesting. Maybe she would read it later. She dropped it on the bed — and found that it fell open about one third of the way through. She looked at the well-thumbed pages and began to read.

It was a section about various herbs and vegetation that were used for medicinal purposes, with suggestions about others that were probably used for what might politely be described as recreational purposes.

Amy was fascinated. She had heard that the South American Indians brewed drinks from herbs and cactus, and their use of herbal cures was well known. Was this what her father was working on? Some sort of herbal product? But why had he been selected for this task when he wasn't a specialist in the subject? It made no sense at all.

She tried to think if she had ever heard him mention working on this sort of thing, but she couldn't.

She looked again at the other book and dropped that on to the bed to see if it fell open at an appropriate page. It didn't.

'Anything interesting?' Greg asked as he came into the room, fresh from his shower. He put an arm round her shoulders, winking as he did so and glancing up at the camera. If they were to be convincing as a newly-engaged couple, they should show a little affection.

'Not especially,' she replied cautiously and pointed at the section she had been reading.

Greg picked it up and read it himself, while Amy looked again at the book on biology. She came to a section on metabolism and thought it looked quite grubby, as if someone had spent considerable time reading it and fingering the pages.

She looked inside the cover to see if there was any indication of the owner of the book. It certainly wasn't one of her father's. There must be some link between the books, and her dad was making some hint about the work he was doing. But it was so frustrating not to be able to share their ideas without being overheard.

'Remember that game we used to play?' Greg asked suddenly. 'Where we drew letters on each other's backs and tried to work out what the message was?'

'Ye-es,' she said doubtfully.

'I've got something to tell you,' he said softly with a smile on his face. 'Go on — guess what I'm saying.' He drew out the letters with his finger on her hand.

'I-L-O-V-E-Y-O-U,' she worked out. 'Oh, Greg.'

'Your turn,' he said, nodding. She realised what he wanted her to do. They could make some comments without being overheard, and as long as they said something after letters had been spelled out, it would look as if they were simply swapping endearments.

Through a combination of writing letters in his hand and pointing at words in the book, she managed to convey that she thought her father was working on some herbal product to do with metabolism.

'Sweetheart,' he replied. 'That's so nice of you. Give me your hand.'

'L-A-B?' he wrote.

'You say the nicest things,' she replied, and nodded.

★   ★   ★

It seemed another long morning, and although they spent some time reading, both of them were frustrated at having nothing more to do. By one o'clock they were becoming irritable and hungry again.

'I know we've done nothing today but I'm starving,' Greg said miserably. 'Yesterday's lack of food must be catching up with me.'

'You never did manage long periods without a square meal.'

'My metabolism,' he said suggestively.

'It's a good job we don't all have the same one.'

'Interesting, isn't it? For so much of

our lives we eat non-stop and never put on a pound, then as we get older, one extra biscuit puts inches on the waistline.'

Greg was thoughtful. Maybe this was it — Jeremy was working on something that speeded up the metabolism, a painless cure for obesity.

He picked up the books again and looked at the pictures, then read some more about the South American Indians. The remote tribe featured in the chapter were all skinny, which he'd assumed was because they had a meagre diet, but perhaps they actually did have some sort of herbal product that prevented them from getting fat.

Wanting to explain his theory to Amy without being watched or overheard, he took her hand and led her into the bathroom, where he flushed the loo and ran the tap, whispering his theory to her as the water ran and masked his words.

'We don't have long before they come down to see what's going on. We can pretend we wanted to smooch without being seen,' he muttered. 'I think this is it — your father's working on some sort of slimming product. That would make sense — he's an expert in his field, and with his intelligence it wouldn't take him long to work it out. Anyone producing a pill from some cheap old herbs to cure obesity will stand to make an absolute fortune.'

'But why go to these lengths? There must be dozens of places where they could develop this sort of thing without all this cloak and dagger carry on. And I didn't notice a computer in his room.'

'I can't explain that. Hang on — someone's coming.'

They were just coming out of the bathroom when an angry looking Juan came into the room.

'What are you doing? Why do you spend so much time in bathroom?'

'We wanted a private kiss. I'm sure you have us under surveillance in here and we wanted privacy.'

'Tidy yourselves and come upstairs. Señor Parra-Moreno invites you to dine with them. It is an honour for you and you will behave appropriately, please.'

Amy combed her hair and fluffed it with her fingers, rubbed at her pale cheeks and smoothed her T-shirt. Greg was wearing a pair of shorts that had seen better days but he made no attempt to 'tidy himself', as Juan had put it.

*　*　*

Juan ushered them up the stairs and indicated the route they should take. They found themselves in the large entrance hall they had seen on the first night, where they were shown into a vast sitting-room. Carved wooden furniture dominated the room, with comfortable sofas and easy chairs dotted around. Low tables held flower arrangements, and several modern paintings hung on the walls. The shutters were partially closed against the bright sunlight outside.

'I'm sure I've seen prints of some of

these,' Amy said of the art without thinking. 'But these most certainly aren't prints. They look like the real thing.'

'You are quite correct, señorita,' a voice said from the shadows. 'I have only originals on my walls. Allow me to introduce myself. I am Ignacio Parra-Moreno. This is my villa where you are my guests.'

The large man who had spoken stepped forward. He was easily as tall as Greg but broader and more powerful looking. He had sleek, dark hair and soft brown eyes that looked almost black in the gloomy light. It was difficult to guess at his age but Amy placed him at around fifty.

'Guests? Prisoners, more like,' Greg burst out. 'Why are you keeping us here? And why is Amy's father a prisoner and being forced to work for you?'

The Spaniard laughed at him. He had an almost gentle sounding laugh, confident and secure that he was fully in charge.

'You are being harsh in your judgement. I am certain that Juan told you that you may leave at any time. We will see you on to the first available flight.'

'Only if Amy and her father come with me,' Greg snapped.

'Sadly that is not possible. Mr Poolley has work to complete and is benefitting from the peace and seclusion of my home. He is not a 'prisoner', as you put it, but my guest. He chooses to work in isolation because he needs to concentrate.'

'But Juan sounded very threatening when he took me to see him,' Amy pointed out. 'He said Dad might see me again only if he worked hard. That hardly sounds like he's some honoured guest in your home.'

'Juan can be — how shall I say? A little over enthusiastic in his work.'

The maid came into the room and spoke in Spanish.

'Lunch is served,' the señor told them. 'Follow me, please.'

Greg took her hand and gripped it hard.

'Keep your temper,' she whispered to him. 'We'll do better if you do.'

'Please, you will sit on my right,' he said to Amy. 'And you, Greg, will sit on my other side. I understand you are recently engaged? Congratulations. But I notice you do not wear a ring. Is it not the custom in England to wear an engagement ring? To show other men that you are taken?'

'We haven't spoken to my father yet,' Amy told him. 'It's the custom for the man to speak to the girl's father first.'

'How old fashioned. I had believed you British women were more independent than that.'

'Not all of us.' Amy smiled sweetly.

The maid served the meal. There were various cooked meats served with fresh bread, pretty much as they had eaten the previous day. This time, it was more graciously served, with heavy silver cutlery and crystal wine glasses to drink from.

The plates were removed and fresh ones laid. A huge fish on a silver platter was distributed, garnished with curls of herbs and wedges of lemon. The conversation was trivial and any attempt to turn it to the serious situation was avoided.

After the fish came a salad, to be followed by a leg of lamb, gently steamed and succulently tender. Greg certainly couldn't complain that he was short of food today. There were pieces of potato that had been fried to a golden brown, and sprinkled with fresh chopped herbs. It all smelled wonderful.

'You like this wine?' They both nodded with enthusiasm, having smelled it first and decided there was nothing untoward about it. 'It is from my own vineyard a few miles away. With the olives, a few vegetables grown locally and our own wine, we are almost self sufficient. There is plenty more. I want to reassure you that you are welcome here.'

'Is my father having lunch?' Amy asked.

'He prefers to eat in the evening. After his work is finished for the day,' she was told.

'And does he share his meal with someone or eat alone in his workshop?'

'Usually he prefers to eat alone so that he can continue with his tasks. Once the work is finished, he will be free to leave and return to his home.'

'Ah, so he *is* being *held* here,' Greg said triumphantly.

'Not at all, but I have hopes that he will finish soon.'

'And exactly what is it he's doing for you?'

'He works for the benefit of the world. Yes, he is producing something that will benefit the whole world.'

'And make you a fortune on the way, I suspect.'

'I have made a large investment — naturally I expect a fair return. Now, if you have had sufficient to eat, we can retire to the terrace for coffee. Come,

Amy, my dear — do you prefer sun or shade?'

Although Ignacio was ostensibly the perfect host, there was something unpleasant about him and the way he spoke. He was clearly not used to being challenged in any way and had an aura of ruthless power about him. Clearly he was a rich and successful man, but how he had become rich left Amy in some doubt. She suspected it might not have been by an entirely honest route.

'So what exactly is this wonderful project my father is working on?' she probed.

'You will be told when it is completed.'

'I need to use the bathroom,' Greg announced. 'I assume there is one nearby?'

'Of course. Juan will show you the way.' The señor clicked his fingers and Juan appeared instantly. Clearly he had been waiting in the background, probably listening to every word that was said.

Amy was left alone with her host.

'Please, why are you keeping us here? My father looks unwell and I need to spend time with him, to see exactly what is wrong with him. And Greg and I need to be able to speak without being overheard. Have you any idea how it feels to be monitored all the time?'

'I am sorry it troubles you, but it is a matter of security from the world. There are many who want to get their hands on the secret work we are doing and I cannot risk my investment.'

'And will my father get anything out of this?'

'Hopefully we shall all benefit. He will be rewarded, never fear. Now, unless there is anything else I can get for you, I will have Juan take you back to your room. I hope you have enjoyed your lunch?'

'It was very nice, thank you. It's a relief to know there can be some civilisation in such a remote place.' She hoped he picked up on her veiled comment. 'Should I wait for Greg?'

'He has already returned to your rooms.'

'When can I see my father again?'

'Later. Now, I will take my leave of you.'

And as he left the room, she was hustled back to her quarters by the over enthusiastic Juan.

★ ★ ★

When Amy got back to their rooms, Greg was already waiting. He looked furious.

'I was practically frogmarched here,' he said angrily. 'I wanted to see something of the house before I was dragged back. Did anything more happen after I left?'

'No, just pleasantries,' she muttered, her eyes rising to the light and its hidden camera and microphone. 'I asked when I could see Dad and the señor said maybe this evening. How on earth he can claim that we're not being held prisoner here, I don't know. But at least it was a good lunch.'

'Splendid. Very civilised. But not exactly the sort of treatment one might expect for so-called guests. Clearly Juan was only inches away the whole time. I'm not sure what we should do next. Maybe I should leave?' He put his arms round her and pretended to kiss her. 'I could always come back and get you out,' he breathed into her ear.

'I doubt if they'd let you off the plane again. Besides, I don't want to be parted from you. I'd go mad in here all by myself.'

After the large lunch, the wine and the inactivity, both felt very sleepy. The day was hot and the usual light breeze was missing. They both fell asleep and didn't wake until it was almost dark. Amy sat up with a start, not knowing where she was. Greg opened his eyes and also sat up.

'We must have slept for ages,' he said.

'Too much food and wine at lunch-time and in this heat. What time is it?'

'Seven-thirty. Seems to get dark early, doesn't it? I'll put the light on.'

'No, don't. The room will be invaded by insects. Besides, it's cosy in the dark.' She nestled closer to him and whispered in his ear, 'We need to talk without being overheard.' Greg put his arm round her and pulled her close. She rather liked it.

'Somehow I need to send a text to London, but how can I do it without being overheard or giving away the fact that I have a mobile?' she murmured.

'I hoped to use mine when I visited a bathroom but that was foiled too,' Greg told her.

'And there's no signal in the bathroom here,' she added. 'I need to get outside somehow. I wonder . . . do you think if I leaned out of the window, I could somehow speak when they call back?'

He shook his head. 'It's not worth risking your phone being taken off you. Would we get away with another migraine? You could have one this time

149

and slip out when supper arrives.'

She rolled away from him and spoke normally again. 'Do you think we're getting any supper tonight? Maybe after that super lunch, they think we don't need any more food. But he did promise I might see Dad again this evening.'

Realising her intention, Greg also spoke up.

'I'll starve if we don't have anything. And I'm really thirsty. The bathroom water tastes funny — I just hope it really is drinkable. I don't fancy getting a serious stomach upset here.'

A few minutes later, they heard the bolt on the door being drawn back and Juan arrived.

'You may see your father now. The señor has agreed that you may dine with him. Something will be brought down here for you,' he added to Greg.

'I don't want special treatment. Why don't I just go with Amy and see her dad?'

'No. You will stay here. Unless you

have decided to return to England?'

'Only if my fiancée and her father can come too.'

'Then you will be staying here. Come,' he ordered Amy.

*   *   *

She went with him, watching as the door was bolted again from the outside, then following him through the garden to the outbuilding that housed her father. She glanced around, trying to see the terrace where they'd sat after lunch, but it must have been on the other side of the house. She was aware of the security belt with her mobile in it, hidden inside her trousers. If only she could find somewhere to use it!

The door was unlocked and her father was waiting inside.

'Oh, Amy, it's so good to see you again!' He hugged her close and seemed a little more relaxed this time, she thought.

'We're actually being allowed to have

a meal together, I think,' she told him.

'That's great. We can catch up a bit, though I expect the conversation will be monitored as usual.'

'I'm not sure why everything we say and do is so interesting to everyone,' she said a tad sharply.

Her father shrugged and gave a wan smile. 'A certain type of neurosis, I expect. A fear of missing out on something vital.'

'So, can you tell me what it is you're working on? I'd have thought biological sciences were out of your league.' She faintly indicated the bookshelves, and he understood that she had figured out what he was trying to tell her by giving her the books he had.

'Yes, my talents are limited,' he agreed, 'but most of my work is being done on computer. It makes testing very much quicker. There's a lot more of the work being carried out in a laboratory elsewhere.'

'I hadn't noticed a computer here,' she said, but before he could reply they were interrupted by the arrival of dinner. It was a simple meal and nothing like the extravaganza she and Greg had enjoyed at lunch-time. In fact, she wasn't at all hungry and she picked at her plate of food, while watching her father eat. She had forgotten his habit of cutting it into small pieces and putting a selection of foods on his fork. He always chewed thoroughly, too, as if thinking deeply all the time.

'I've missed you,' she said suddenly. 'And I've been worried about you. How much longer will you be working here?'

'I don't know. I'm not sure what else they want me to do. I had a lot of work to complete before . . . well, before I came away. Doubtless my office will be concerned.' He was looking at her in a strange way, wondering if she would tell him anything and almost warning her against it.

'I expect they knew you were taking some leave for my holiday,' she assured him with a slight nod, and he understood that she had indeed been in contact with them. 'It was very sudden, wasn't it? I only spoke with you on the Sunday and you must have gone away soon after that.'

'Almost as soon as we'd spoken. I tried to leave you a note but I was accompanied all the way and had no opportunity to let you know. I'm sorry — it must have been a shock to you.'

'I did find a note. But I was very worried — I couldn't just stay at home waiting to hear something. Pamela and Henry were wonderful. Anyway, you said you're working with a computer?' He nodded. 'So you do have a computer here? Do you have internet access.'

He nodded. 'But it's only under supervision, in case I try to make contact with anyone.'

The door was flung open and a furious Juan rushed in.

'That is enough! You agreed to say nothing of consequence to your daughter. You have abused our trust! Now you will not see her until the next phase of the work is completed. Come,' he said, gripping Amy firmly by the arm, 'you will return to your room . . . and don't expect any more consideration.'

She was half dragged back along the paths and bundled down the stairs again. She almost fell into the bedroom.

Greg leapt to his feet in concern. 'Amy, are you all right?'

'Yes. Evidently Dad was saying a bit too much to me and Juan got twitchy. I assume they thought it might be some sort of security risk. I think our suppositions were right, though, about his work. I just don't know how long it's all going to take. I'll go crazy if we're kept here for much longer.' As she burst into tears of distress, Greg put his arms round her and held her.

'It's all right, love, we'll get out, I promise you. There has to be a way.' He stroked her hair gently. 'Amy, I . . . '

'Shhh,' she hissed. 'Remember big brother,' she said and flicked her eyes to the camera for a second.

'I've been having thoughts about your brother,' Greg said meaningly. 'I was thinking that he might worry if you're out of contact altogether, but for a few minutes at least, it might be worth it.'

'Sabotage?' she whispered close by his ear.

'Exactly.' He kissed her and touched her cheek. 'This could become habit forming,' he murmured.

'I agree.' They stood by the window and looked out into the blackness. There were stars in the sky, shining brightly, with no light pollution to spoil the view.

'You never see stars like this in a city. I'll turn the light out so we can see them better,' Amy commented loudly, and crossed to the switch. Immediately Greg leapt up on the bed and hit the camera with his shoe. He bashed it till he was satisfied it wasn't working and Amy pulled her phone from its hiding place.

'Call that number quick. We don't

have long before they realise what we've done and come rushing down. I'll jam the door somehow in case they try to rush in.'

She wrote the word BUZZARD and sent it to the number she had saved in her phone. Seconds later the phone vibrated silently.

'Hello? It's Amy. You must listen — I have only a moment. We're being kept in a villa in the mountains above Mojácar in Spain. The village is called Las Minas, and we're about two kilometres outside it. My father is being made to work on some project to develop a new drug, we think. Something to do with slimming, perhaps.'

'Do you have the names of any of your captors?'

'Ignacio Parra-Moreno. His henchman is called Juan — but I s'pose so are millions of others in Spain.'

'OK. Is your father being ill-treated in any way? Drugged, or being forced to say or do anything against his will?'

'I don't think so, unless you count

working for nothing and being kept locked in a small building all the time. Evidently I was brought here to ensure his co-operation. We're being kept prisoner — ' There was a crashing noise from outside the door as someone came rushing down the stairs.

'Gotta go! My phone's turned off most of the time. I keep it hidden.' She switched it off and stuffed it back into her pouch, tucking it well down in her trousers.

'Well done,' Greg whispered. 'Now quick, get into bed. We can pretend we wanted privacy and I flung my shoe at the camera.'

There was more banging before the door gave way and Juan and another swarthy looking man rushed into the room, trying to switch on the light as they did so. They carried torches and shone them at the bed.

'Exactly what is going on?' Juan yelled. The light steamed in from behind him.

'We wanted some privacy,' Greg said

calmly. 'We didn't want to be spied on while we . . . ' He paused suggestively.

'So, your high morals are not so high after all,' Juan said with a leer. 'But you will pay for damaging the señor's property. If you wish to share a bed, you will do so under our surveillance.' He pointed threateningly at Amy. 'Otherwise, you will spend your time alone.'

'Sorry. Greg didn't realise he was such a good shot. He threw his shoe at the light and hit it fair and square. We're sorry.'

'Go into the other room. This light will have to be repaired.'

'OK, but please wait outside until we're dressed.' Greg didn't want the men to see that they were both fully clad and so reveal their bluff.

After a moment's hesitation the two men moved back towards the door and turned away.

Feeling slightly hysterical, Amy got the giggles while she pretended to pull on her trousers and shirt. Greg squeezed her hand, and finally they both stood up.

'Right. So, you want us in the other room?' he asked.

'Move it,' snapped Juan.

'Your English is very good,' Greg remarked conversationally. 'You know all the right phrases; it must be from watching British television.'

The second man snarled at him and made as if to hit him, but Juan calmed him with a few words of Spanish. They almost shoved Amy and Greg into the other room and locked the one they had been using.

'My things are all in there,' Amy protested.

'You'll get them tomorrow. Now settle down and be quiet for the rest of the night,' Juan commanded.

'Sleep well,' Greg called after them. 'And good riddance,' he muttered.

'I assume big brother's back with us.'

'I guess so. There's no need to pretend we don't know about it any more, though.' He gave a wave to the camera before switching off the light and settling down.

'Don't worry. Your honour's safe with me,' he assured her, and they both laughed as they fell into an exhausted sleep, wrapped in each other's arms.

★ ★ ★

They awoke in the morning to the sounds of drilling and people talking.

'Sounds like they're mending our broken light,' Greg said as he sat up. 'Is it OK if I use the bathroom first?'

'Of course. I need some clean things out of my rucksack anyway.'

She sat on the bed, her arms round her knees, wondering if the message she had managed to get out would achieve anything. Not that she could imagine what might be done. Her father's office had already told her they could do nothing to help her, but maybe rescuing Jeremy was another matter. Perhaps they were scared that he might be forced to tell some secret or other. Not that she knew if he had any secrets to tell.

What a mess it all was! They had to do something, but what? They were so far from anywhere that an escape on foot wasn't practical, and she would bet that the señor was a well respected member of the community. Nobody would believe that he was holding people prisoner.

She heard Greg's shower ending and went to the door to her room.

'Excuse me. May I collect my bag?' she asked the workman standing on a stepladder in the middle of the room. He shrugged, not understanding. She pointed at her rucksack, and he shrugged again. Clearly he spoke no English and couldn't care less what she did.

He had a walkie-talkie in his hand and spoke rapidly into it, then adjusted the miniature camera in the light fitting and spoke again. It appeared to be working, so he pocketed his tools and came down from the ladder. He spoke to Amy in another torrent of Spanish, but she shook her head to indicate that she did not understand.

'Everything all right?' Greg asked as he came in, wet hair dripping.

'I'm just collecting my things. I was thinking, I might wash out a few things. I expect they'll dry by the window.'

'Good idea. I've got some smelly socks and stuff myself.'

Once she had showered and dressed, breakfast arrived. They ate in silence and then went into the bathroom, ostensibly to wash out their clothes.

'This was a brilliant idea — we can chat for a few minutes in peace,' Greg said. 'I think we need to make a plan. I might try to escape down to the village and at least make some calls. It means leaving you but I don't think they'll try anything drastic until your father has completed whatever it is he's doing. I need that phone number of yours and I can try using your code word. It may not work since the number I'll be dialling from is different. Can you manage alone for a while, do you think?'

'I s'pose so. I'll miss you though.'

'It won't be for long. Once I'm in the village, there must be someone who'll be able to help us.'

'Take care though — I bet he's got at least some of the villagers on his pay roll. How will you do it?'

'I'll hide in here behind the door, just as we hear the door being unbolted, so that nobody will notice before that that I'm not in visual range. Then a quick dash up the steps and I'll hide till it's quite dark. Then over the wall and away.'

'You make it sound so easy! We'd better finish here or they'll get suspicious all over again.'

They took their dripping clothes and hung them over the curtain rail. With the window open as wide as possible, they would dry.

★   ★   ★

It was another long, boring day. There was no lunch invitation to break the monotony and though a meal was brought, it was only another selection of cold meats and salad.

Their plan was to be initiated when dinner was brought to them. They assumed that their antics last night would mean no visit to Jeremy, but at least they were prepared and had some sort of plan.

Amy picked up one of the books again and read some more about the South American Indians.

'It's quite amazing to think that there could still be places deep in the Amazon rain forests that have never been discovered. You'd think with planes and helicopters, nothing could remain hidden.'

'It's a vast area. There must be places where a plane has never flown. Besides, the trees are so dense, they wouldn't see anything below the canopy anyhow. Your tribe has been discovered though — there are photographs to prove it.'

'Listen to this. 'We were invited to share a feast with the tribe in return for giving them things we had with us; simple items of clothing, paper, and we showed them how to use charcoal to make pictures. I even gave the chief a penknife, something I hope not to regret at a later date! The feast was splendid. Their ability to nurture animals for the table, and the many plants and herbs, some of them extremely rare, they used for flavouring was quite remarkable. I am certain that the food would be quite acceptable in the best restaurants in London or Paris.' Interesting, isn't it?'

'A whole community tucked away from the world. I wonder how they communicated with their visitors?'

'Miming, I suppose. I bet they didn't use computer translations.'

'So when was that written?'

'The book was published in the twenties. It's based on someone's diaries, but I think the actual explorer must have lived much earlier.' Amy looked back at the title pages. 'I suppose there's some hint of this particular herb in here. I can't imagine how the association was made though.'

'Maybe there are more records somewhere. Perhaps someone new has been exploring,' Greg suggested. 'Maybe it's in one of the areas that are being carved up at present. They keep blaming climate change on the destruction of the rain forest, but still the forests continue to be decimated.'

'There are companies who send people out looking for the herbs and things. But, you know, we're not even certain that this is the real clue to what's going on — though Dad hinted at it last night.' She sighed. 'This was supposed to be a nice holiday and time spent catching up with Dad. We'd even planned to walk part of the Cornish Coastal path.'

'That's a good thing to do. Look, I'm going to do some exercises if you don't mind. I'm beginning to feel desperately unfit with all this sitting around.'

He began to do some stretches to warm up and then gradually built up various strenuous-looking exercises that made Amy feel tired just watching.

'I can't do all my usual stuff without any equipment,' he grunted.

'You look as if you're doing all right to me,' she said on a laugh.

'I usually work out a few times a week, but I haven't done anything since our little jog on Sunday.'

'That seems a lifetime ago. What day is it? Only Thursday?'

'I expect my parents will be wondering what's happening, but there's no way I can let them know where we are. I just hope they don't contact the police or anything. They know exactly the place we were coming to.'

'Well, maybe, roughly where we are. It's a big area.'

'Don't forget there are records of when we arrived, and there's the hotel we stayed in the first night. I paid by credit card so there will be a record of that.' She realised that Greg was doing his best to worry their guards behind the surveillance cameras and played along.

'Yes, of course. They wanted to see our passports and everything, didn't they? And they have our home addresses. Yes, you're right, plenty of people would know where to start looking. Now, are you going to stop jigging around? You're making me feel giddy.'

'I wonder if our gracious hosts are going to allow us or you to see your father this evening? And if we're getting any dinner at all?' Greg grumbled. 'I'm starving.'

'You always are.' As she spoke, they heard the door open on the stairs.

'Heavens,' Greg grunted. 'I think I'm going to be sick — ' As they had planned, Greg rushed into the bathroom and splashed some water around just as Juan arrived in the room with the maid.

'Your meal. You will not be seeing your father this evening.'

Amy knew she needed to make some

sort of diversion to allow Greg the best chance she could. He had left the bathroom door slightly open so that he could slip out without making a noise, but they hadn't bargained on having both the maid and Juan arrive together.

'That is so unfair,' she almost shouted. 'I was longing to see my dad. We haven't been together for ages. It isn't easy to talk with you lot watching and listening in on everything.' She sounded slightly hysterical and was stamping her feet at the same time.

'Behave yourself. You're just a spoilt brat, aren't you? Spanish women would never behave like that.'

'Yes, well, I'm not a Spanish woman, I'm English, and I want to go home with my father and get back to our normal lives.'

'Be quiet.' He raised a hand as though to slap her and she retreated quickly towards the window.

'Don't you dare hit me!' she screamed.

'I see your man doesn't come to defend you.'

'He's unwell,' she said quickly. 'He has a bad stomach — probably due to being imprisoned here with its rotten water.'

'I keep telling you, he is not imprisoned, as you put it. Nor are you. You are being offered hospitality. You can go home whenever you like. Stop making such a fuss.'

'Go on, you,' he muttered to the maid as she stood by the door, looking worried. He repeated his command in Spanish and she turned to flee up the stairs. He followed without checking the bathroom.

Amy peered round the bathroom door.

'Are you feeling better?' she said to the empty room.

She made some grunting noises and turned off the taps.

'OK then. I'll get my meal, if that's all right. I'll leave yours in case you want it later.'

With her fingers tightly crossed, she hoped he had escaped.

A Tense Evening

Though she didn't feel much like food, Amy forced herself to eat the meal that had been brought. Poor Greg — he'd had to go without and that wouldn't please him.

Several times she got up for the benefit of the camera and asked through the bathroom door how he was feeling.

'That's a good idea. You go straight to bed,' she called.

She switched off the lights then opened and shut the doors, as if it was indeed Greg going to bed.

'Night. Hope you feel better tomorrow.'

In the darkness, she stuffed the pillows and some clothes in the bed, to look as if it was Greg asleep under the covers.

Back in her own room, she put the

tray near the door and turned off the light so that she could open the window. She could see no sign of anyone in the grounds. 'I hope you make it,' she willed silently to Greg in the darkness. She was missing his large, comforting presence already. Despite knowing him practically all her life, he had become something much more in this past week. Maybe it was just the circumstances, but he was now very special to her. Only a week. It was hard to believe everything that had happened in so short a time. I'm falling in love with him, she realised suddenly. Dear Greg.

As she stared out, she thought she caught a movement among the bushes. Leaning against the window, peering to one side, she hoped to catch a glimpse of something . . . anything. There was a sudden flash as a spotlight came on, triggered by some movement. 'Oh no, don't let it be Greg,' she breathed.

She heard a dog bark and the sound of running feet, and her heart sank. Her breathing sounding louder than any of the night noises outside, she waited, expecting him to be brought back at any second. But everything remained quiet. The security lights flashed on and off, but she could see nothing.

If they had caught Greg, perhaps they would keep him somewhere else and not let him return to her.

Even if he hadn't been caught, she couldn't keep his absence a secret after dawn the next day.

At last she lay on the bed and tried to sleep, but her frenzied mind raced on, round and round. What could be the eventual outcome? Once her father's work was completed, what would happen to them all? If it was something illegal, their captors, as she was thinking of them, could hardly just let them go. Would they meet some sticky end here?

Wherever her thoughts led her, she didn't like the possibilities. It was all down to Greg from now on.

★ ★ ★

As silently as he could, Greg slipped up the stairs. The heavy door at the top was pushed to and he heard Amy begin her noisy outburst as he reached it. Good girl, he thought. He opened it almost silently and went through into the long passage. He had no idea how long he had before Juan and the maid came up, so he hid in one of the other doorways, praying that they wouldn't pass the same way.

His stomach grumbled, as it always did when he was hungry, and he hoped he wouldn't be given away by something so silly.

As he heard them coming up the stairs, he pressed himself into the doorway and held his breath. They bolted the door from the outside and went back towards the main part of the house.

Quietly he opened the door where he was hiding and looked into the room. It was another bedroom. The bed wasn't made. He tiptoed to the window and looked out. It was a simple matter to open it and step over the sill and on to the balcony below. It was much easier than his previous excursion when he'd gone right through the house in great fear of being discovered at any moment.

He climbed down to the ground, cursing the steep site that made it necessary to build on so many different levels. He looked across to the windows he assumed to be their rooms, but it was way out of reach. Should he go back to the stairs and try to get Amy out as well? But he quickly decided against that plan; he stood more chance of getting help if he was on his own. Once he was out of earshot of the house, he could use his own mobile phone and try to get help. If that failed, he could go down to the village to seek help there.

As his eyes became accustomed to the dark he began to make out shapes in the garden. On this side, it fell away steeply and he could make out some sort of fence or hedge at the bottom. The steep walls of the building rose behind him and that meant the main garden, terraces and pool were behind the house on the other side. He descended cautiously, aware that there were bushes and cacti growing everywhere, and plenty of loose stones which made a noise if he stood on them.

At one point, he lost his footing and slid some distance down the slope.

Suddenly the darkness was broken by a powerful floodlight shining over the garden. He pressed himself flat against the ground and lay still, hardly daring to breathe as he heard raised voices and waited for his inevitable capture.

The barking of dogs set his heart pounding but he stayed in place, rigid with fear.

Presently he heard the men retreating back to the house and the light went out. Whatever had set the alarm off, it wasn't him.

Cautiously he got up and crept further down the hillside to the wall, where he sheltered in its shadow and waited for his heart to still again. He could see that the wall was topped with vicious looking razor wire, and almost impossible to climb over, and he cursed silently. Feeling in one of his many pockets, he pulled out the folded survival blanket he'd stuffed in just in case. It was made of foil and not very strong but it might just be enough to protect him from the worst.

He managed to find foot and hand holds and climbed up to the top where he shook out the blanket, very aware of the slight noise it made and the bright reflection in the moonlight, and scrambled over the wire. He felt the odd nick as he went but the adrenaline was flowing and he barely stopped except to remove what was left of the foil from the top of the wall and stuff it back into his pocket. He might need it again.

There was only one way to go and that was down. He found the road and began to jog down it, taking care not to slip on the loose stones. When he heard a vehicle approaching, the strange acoustics of the mountainside meant he wasn't sure if it was coming up or down, so just in case it was someone looking for him, he stepped off the road and hid. From this vantage point he saw that it was the same Freelander that had brought them here; now it was again going up to the villa. He couldn't see who was driving.

Once it was out of sight, he began the descent once more.

After a while, he stopped for a rest and took out his mobile phone. He typed the word BUZZARD on his keypad and sent it to the number Amy had given him. It was quickly answered and the voice was querulous.

'Who is this?'

'My name is Greg Harvey. I'm Amy Poolley's companion.'

'I'm sorry — you have the wrong number.'

'No, please listen! She called you earlier and told you that we're being held captive in a villa near the village of Las Minas, outside Mojácar. Her father is Jeremy Poolley. Her mother died when she was a tiny baby. She's been in France for the past year and just came home. What else can I tell you?'

'Do you know the name of her first kitten?'

'Winkie. I'm sure it was Winkie.'

'When did she get her first bicycle?'

'Oh, for heaven's sake — when she was six. It was a red one and she got it for her birthday. Now can we get on, please?'

There was a pause.

'You were with her when she last called?'

'Yes, right beside her. It was last night. She told you we're being held in a villa in the mountains. I've made a break for it but I've had to leave Amy and her father behind. We're under constant video surveillance in our rooms.'

'So how did you manage to retain your mobiles?'

'I had put a spare one in my pack, which they took, and we both kept the ones we've used hidden in our clothes.'

'What exactly are you hoping to achieve by contacting us?'

'I don't know. To get us some help, to get us away?'

'I warned Amy that any journey she made was at her own risk.'

'I know, but we really need some help. All of us. Even if I could, I daren't drag Amy outside the villa and leave her father a prisoner there.'

'You're absolutely certain he's being kept against his will?'

'Of course! Don't you have somebody here you can send in? Some agent on the ground, as it were?'

'I'm not quite sure what you think we are, Mr Harvey. This isn't some sort of spy ring. It's a business organisation. Mr Poolley works for us.'

'Then why all the security? The code words and identity stuff?'

'Industrial espionage is big business. There's a lot of money involved.'

'Look, can you help or not? I don't know how long I've got before I'm discovered. Hopefully I've got till morning but my absence might be noticed earlier, and I'm not sure if Amy or her father will be safe once they realise I've got away.'

He was continuing down the mountainside as he was talking and now he was almost at the edge of the village.

'Aren't you the British Government?' he probed.

'Of course not!'

'Then who are you? I thought Jeremy worked for the Government. Official Secrets Act and everything.'

'He may have done at one time, but not now,' he was told coolly. 'Can you tell us anything about the work he is doing for these people?'

'Not really. It's some sort of research work. He wasn't able to tell Amy much but he gave her some books to read. We're only guessing at what he's doing, but it may be something to do with a herbal drug — possibly some sort of weight reduction product. Come on now — I've told you everything I can. We need help!'

'If you can get to Mojácar and call me from there, I'll try to organise some help for you,' the voice conceded. 'There is a currency exchange office there. I'll see that a message is left there for you.'

'And if I fail?'

'I'll do what I can.' And the connection was broken.

Greg looked helplessly at his mobile. The battery was beginning to get low, yet he needed to keep it switched on in case Amy tried to call or this office place, whatever it was, called back.

The village he had reached was mainly a residential place with one or two bars and a couple of small shops. Everything seemed closer. A few lights shone through shutters, but the place seemed deserted. He walked to the other end, still not sure what he should do. He could hardly knock on someone's door and tell his story! It was too dangerous, and anyway, these people might work for the señor.

He wondered if he had the energy to

walk or jog to Mojácar. Though it could be seen in the distance, it had seemed quite a long drive, and in the dark, it would be easy to lose the way. But he had little alternative. Unless he was to be locked up again, he had to make an attempt to reach the town. At a fairly slow pace, he began to run . . .

The track had become a proper tarred road and he was able to run with confidence. He glanced at his watch — almost midnight. He hoped Amy was managing to sleep and that it wouldn't be long before they were back together.

At about two o'clock, he stopped for a rest behind a wall. He was feeling very thirsty but he could see no chance of finding drinking water and wished he had thought to bring some with him.

Occasionally a vehicle had passed him but after the first two or three, he had given up trying to hide. If they hadn't sent someone to search for him soon after midnight, he clearly hadn't been missed. Hopefully Amy had managed to keep up the pretence that he was ill, and in the darkness, the cameras wouldn't have missed him. As he leaned against the wall, feeling exhausted, his eyes grew heavy and he slipped into a deep sleep . . .

He awoke with a jolt as daylight was breaking and scrambled to his feet. As soon as it was properly light, he would be missed and they would certainly send someone after him. He rubbed his stiff and aching muscles and slowly began to run again . . .

He passed through another village. There was a pump to one side of the road and he pumped the handle, letting the cold water run over his head. He drank only a tiny amount, just to moisten his dry mouth, praying that the water was safe. A lorry ground its way along the road and slowed down, the driver calling out something, slowing as he passed, but Greg couldn't understand.

'Mojácar?' he called back hopefully.

'Nah,' the driver said with a shake of the head and accelerated away.

A little further ahead, the road split

into two. Greg looked at the still distant town and decided that it seemed as if either route would take him into the town, so he took a chance and plumped for the one that looked flatter.

Another village came into view, and he saw that a small café was open. Knowing that he would make better progress with some food and drink inside him, he managed to order something to eat and some coffee with an elaborate mime to make up for his deficiency in Spanish.

One or two more customers came in and sat at the grubby tables, muttering and smoking evil-smelling cigarettes. The waiter brought his food, a basket of rolls, some jam and butter and a couple of slices of ham. He ate the unappetising fare, seeing it purely as fuel for his journey. The hot coffee was surprisingly good, though, and he drank it quickly.

A bus was coming along the road and he quickly flung down a few euros, calling thanks to the waiter, and dashed out to the bus. He didn't much care where it was going as long as it took him as far away from Las Minas as possible. As it happened it was going to Mojácar and he slumped down in his seat, greatly relieved.

There seemed to be a great number of new houses along the road. Wherever there was a hill, the top had been flattened and a house built. The land was arid and dry but there seemed to be a few colourful flowers struggling to flourish along the roadside. Cactus spikes grew wild, and sandy rocks made small canyons along the dried-out river beds.

The town came into sight at last and Greg breathed a sigh of relief. He wondered if there might be a shop where he could buy another battery for his phone — with luck, one that was ready charged.

However, the first task was to find the currency office, though it might be a bit soon for any message to have been sent.

Though still early, there were a lot of people around, people walking along the promenade taking the air before the heat of the day sent them indoors. There were a number of British people among them and they said a polite good morning as they passed. Greg was tempted to confide his story to someone but dared not risk it. He was becoming quite paranoid in case he might meet anyone who worked for Señor Ignacio Parra-Moreno.

★　★　★

Amy spent a restless night, expecting Greg to be brought back at any time. She had kept up the pretence of him being ill and made several visits to speak to the lumps of pillow lying in his bed. She knew it was only a matter of time before his absence was discovered and she feared the repercussions that might follow. What could they do to her? Or worse, to her father? Clearly they did need him and she couldn't quite believe they would do anything that would actually endanger anyone's life.

She tried to comfort herself with the thought that, whatever else, the señor seemed to be a relatively civilised human being. It was all very strange. More like some novel than reality.

She heard the bolt being drawn back on the big door at the top of the stairs and held her breath. If it was the maid, she might not be suspicious of Greg's absence. If it was Juan, things could get difficult.

She lay back on top of the bed and closed her eyes. Perhaps if she, too, pretended to have a bad stomach, it might look more convincing.

The maid came in with a tray.

'I'm ill,' Amy moaned, clutching her middle.

The maid stared at her uncertainly. Putting the breakfast tray down she peered more closely at the girl, babbled something in Spanish that Amy didn't understand, then turned away to lift the tray from the night before and take it away.

The door wasn't bolted and for a moment Amy considered making a dash for it. But there was no time — very soon, Juan arrived.

'So, what is wrong with you?' he asked curtly.

'Stomach pains. We're probably suffering from food poisoning. Greg was up half the night.' She kept her fingers crossed that he wouldn't investigate the other room.

'Rubbish. You had the same food as the rest of us. Nobody else is affected.'

'Maybe it's the water down here. You could bring us some bottled water. Plenty of it, please.'

'Where is your man?' he demanded.

'He's asleep in his room.' As the Spaniard opened the door and peered inside, Amy held her breath. But he seemed to accept the lump in the bed as being Greg.

'OK. I'll send some bottled water down and maybe some medication.'

Amy began to breathe normally again as he stamped back up the stairs. That had been a close call. She hoped Greg had been able to organise some help. Maybe his absence wouldn't be discovered after all. She risked switching on her mobile, in case he'd left a message, but there was nothing.

It was an hour later before the maid came down with several bottles of water and some pills Amy recognised as an over-the-counter remedy for diarrhoea.

'Thank you,' she murmured, pretending she was still in pain. The maid again muttered something in Spanish and touched her shoulder with a sympathetic gesture.

When she had left, Amy pretended to take one of the pills, and then, for the benefit of the watching camera, went into Greg's room. Making sure she was hiding the 'body' on the bed, she made as if she was giving him the pills and water, chatting to him as if he was there and reassuring him that she was feeling a bit better.

'Lie still. I hope you'll soon feel better, too,' she said, closing the door behind her. She wondered where Greg was now. Had he got away from this mountainside and found help?

If she had been bored and frustrated before, without Greg for company it was a hundred times worse. She read and re-read the two books of her father's. The science book still meant next to nothing to her. The travel book was mildly interesting, but not enough to absorb her. The day dragged on . . .

No more food was brought, which made sense given their present state of 'health'. However, she was beginning to feel quite hungry and nibbled at the now slightly stale rolls from breakfast. She wondered if Greg had managed to find any food yet.

Dear Greg. She felt tears forming. What was she doing here and why couldn't something — *anything* — happen soon?

At last she fell asleep and dreamed impossible dreams.

She awoke as the bolt was being drawn back on the door and for a moment wondered where she was. But then everything flooded back to her as Juan came into the room.

'Are you any better?'

'I suppose so.'

'Then perhaps you would like to eat supper with your father.'

She leapt off the bed in excitement.

'Of course I would! Thank you.'

'And how is your man?'

She gave a start. Greg's absence mustn't be discovered now.

'I think he's better since he had the medication. But he's still asleep.'

'Really?' Juan said, clearly disbelieving her. 'Come on then.'

He led her up the stairs, but when he didn't bolt the door behind them, she wondered if something was wrong. Did they suspect that Greg wasn't there?

She followed him to the little building that housed her father.

'Hello, darling girl,' her dad greeted her with a warm hug. 'Are you feeling better now? They said you were unwell.'

'I'm much better for seeing you. It's seemed like an age.' They hugged and she felt warm and safe with the familiarity of him.

'So what was wrong? And what about Greg?'

'It's a long story. Tell me what's going on with you now.' She gave him a long stare. She knew the listeners would be waiting to hear any comments they could so she dared not even hint at what had really been happening. Yet she would have to try to pass on the news somehow . . .

'I think I'm within sight of the end. It's gone well over the last couple of days. I don't know what else they're expecting of me. In fact, I'm still not sure why they chose me for this project. It's not as if I'm well versed in such science.'

'So, if you're nearly finished, do you think they'll let us go soon?'

'Who knows?' He looked slightly uneasy and Amy wondered if he had some sort of extra worries.

'Now, shall we eat our supper?' he went on. 'I'd like you to tell me all about this romance with you and Greg. It does seem rather sudden.'

What was she to say? There *was* no romance, not really, even though she had almost begun to think of herself as a part of Greg's life.

'It was quite a whirlwind romance. But you know we've always been very close. I love him, Dad, really love him.' Saying the words gave her a warm glow and she realised she really meant them. She just hoped Greg felt the same.

'I expect Pam and Henry are delighted. We often talked of the possibility since when you were first born.'

'This pasta's good,' Amy commented, not wanting to deliberately tell her father untruths. 'I'm starving.'

'If you've been sick, don't eat too much to start with. Your stomach will be inflamed and too much food will give you more pain.'

'I wasn't actually sick,' she said cautiously. 'It was more in sympathy with Greg?' She raised an eyebrow, indicating that he should stop talking about it and he gave the slightest nod.

They ate the rest of the meal and chatted inconsequentially, hoping the listeners would relax a little and allow her to pass on proper messages.

'Do you think we might be allowed a little walk around the garden? I could really do with some air.'

'Maybe. It would be a kindness, wouldn't it? You do look very pale. We'll ask when they come back to collect the tray.'

'Will your office be missing you?' she asked.

'I expect they'll wonder why I haven't checked in. But they did know I was going to have a holiday. Some holiday it turned out to be!'

'At least I'm not wasting leave like Greg is. He took a week off to come with me, thinking we were going to have a nice break in the sun, not be kept cooped up in some millionaire's mansion and locked in like some sort of criminal.'

'Shh,' her father warned. 'Best not to cause too many waves.'

The door opened and Juan came in. 'You can take a walk for a short while. The señor has authorised me to allow you to walk together in the garden. You have twenty minutes but we shall be right behind you, so no tricks.'

Delightedly Amy took her father's arm and they set off into the cool evening air. It was almost dark but the bright moon allowed them to see where they were going.

'Greg's not ill,' she began to whisper rapidly. 'He escaped last night and I've been pretending he's sick in his bed. He has your office number and should have contacted them by now. Though they warned me that they couldn't help me, they'll surely want to rescue you. All your secret work for the Government and everything.' She felt his arm stiffen as she was speaking and he looked most uncomfortable. 'Dad? What's wrong?'

'Nothing, darling, nothing at all. I just hope Greg knows what he's getting into. I hope he hasn't put himself and you in extra danger. Now, speak a little louder about the flowers or something. They'll only be suspicious if we keep mumbling.'

She stared at him. 'There's something wrong, isn't there? Something you're not telling me.'

'No. No, of course not. I'm sure it'll all work out. Look — aren't those roses wonderful? An amazing display in this hot, dry climate.'

Amy felt deflated. She had expected her father to be excited about their daring escape and the prospect of being rescued. Clearly, he wasn't.

They were left to walk around for some time. She was becoming slightly worried by the lack of supervision and wondered why they had suddenly become so lenient.

'Isn't it strange that they've left us alone for so long?' she asked.

'They're not all bad. They've treated me quite well really.'

'I don't call being locked in a room under constant surveillance being 'treated quite well'. What's going on, Dad?'

'Nothing. I'm doing some work for them, that's all. Stop worrying. Everything's fine.'

'But why was I brought here? Why all the veiled threats? That Juan character actually said I was here to encourage you to work harder. That's a threat in my book. And if it's all so above board, why can't we leave?'

'Nothing is ever that straightforward.' He was still speaking quietly. 'I know you've been worried but it will soon be over, I promise you. I may not like what I've been doing but I had no choice at the time.' He raised his voice after this speech. 'We'll soon have our holiday as planned and then we can both get on with the rest of our lives. I wondered if you might like a bit of a tour round Spain, since we're here? Give us time to catch up.'

'And Greg? What about him?'

'He can come, too, if he's got time. I suspect you're worried about him,' he added in an undertone.

'He did leave last night. If he walked all the way to Mojácar, he'd have been there by now. Why haven't we heard something?' she murmured.

They didn't hear Juan coming up behind them and both jumped as he spoke out of the darkness.

'It is time for you to return to your rooms.'

Amy clutched her father's arm and held it tightly.

'It's all right, love,' he reassured her. 'I'll see you tomorrow. Go and get some sleep now.' He kissed her cheek and pushed her away gently.

'But . . . ' she muttered, then gave a shrug. 'OK. Love you, Dad.'

'Me too. Night. And stop worrying.' He went back to his room and waved from the doorway.

Juan took her arm and led her round the side of the building.

'Where are you taking me?' she asked as they went into another entrance to the house. 'Why aren't you taking me back to my room?'

'I have a change of scene for you,' he said with an unpleasant leer.

'But what about my things? And Greg?'

'Let's not play games any more. Your man has left you — abandoned you. Your things are here, in your new room.' He opened a door and almost pushed her inside.

This room was on the same level as the rest of the house and much smaller than the one she'd had before. Her rucksack was on the bed and there were a number of books piled on the bedside table. She glanced around and saw there was a small ensuite bathroom instead of the separate bathroom as in the other place. The window had bars on the outside and only a narrow ventilation slit at the top. Once the door was locked, there was no way out.

She slumped down on the bed and

stared at her jailer. 'So where's Greg?'

'I have no idea. Where do you think he might be?' he returned.

'Hopefully bringing some sort of rescue.'

Juan smiled — an unpleasant smile, more a sort of leer.

'Don't count on that young man bringing any help,' he scoffed. 'I hope you're not too lonely. You have some more harmless books to keep you occupied. Goodnight.' He went out, locking the door as noisily as he could behind him.

'Nasty little man,' she muttered.

She looked around and peered up at the light. She couldn't see any sort of camera hidden there and went round the rest of the room, pushing and poking at anything that might have hidden surveillance equipment. She found nothing, but she didn't think for one minute that she wasn't being watched. What had happened to Greg? And why had her father acted so oddly when she'd talked of rescue? Could things actually be something other than they had thought? Maybe her father wasn't actually being kept a prisoner. Yet it was unthinkable that he would be co-operating with something illegal, if that was what it was.

She shoved her bag off the bed and lay back, trying to come to terms with what was going on. Had Greg been caught again and locked away somewhere else? The uncertainty was almost worse than the previous day of waiting for something to happen. But she mustn't allow herself to give in to despair. She must stay strong at all costs.

Who To Trust?

Greg walked along the streets of the little town, looking for a currency dealer. Finding two, he was in an immediate quandary about which was the correct one. He had no choice but to walk in to the first one and ask if there was a message for Greg Harvey. The girl shook her head.

'For Amy Poolley, then? Or Jeremy Poolley?'

'I'm sorry, sir. We don't operate any sort of messaging service. Can I help you in some other way?'

'No. Thanks. Sorry to bother you. Good morning.' He went out into the now blazing heat and cursed himself for giving away so much. He'd mentioned all their names. Suppose she knew about the situation and was working for the señor? He went along to the next dealer. Perhaps he should draw out some cash of his own in case he needed it.

He opened the door of the next place and went inside. It was blissfully cool with air conditioning that felt wonderful after the hot sun.

'Good, isn't it?' said the young man sitting at the reception desk. 'Everyone gets that look of relief as they come inside. How can I help you?'

'I need some more euros. Can I cash a cheque?'

'I'm sorry, sir, but we only deal with registered clients. If you want to cash travellers' cheques, you need a bank or a money changer.'

'Right. Sorry. I didn't realise places like this existed so I wasn't sure what you did.'

'Lots of Brits live here and need to transfer currency over here from the UK. Can I help in any other way?'

'I wondered if a message has been left for me? Greg Harvey.'

'One moment, sir, and I'll check. Would it be a fax or email, or maybe a letter?'

'I'm not sure. Not a letter. Maybe an email or a fax. Someone said they'd send one to the currency dealer.'

The young man tapped on his computer. 'Greg Harvey, you said? With reference to what?'

'Jeremy or Amy?' he said, not wanting to make the mistake of giving too much away this time.

'Can't see anything here. Can you leave a number with me and I can contact you if anything comes in?'

'I have a mobile but the battery's very low and I don't have a charger. Perhaps you can point me towards a shop where I might get another?'

'There's a store in the shopping complex along the road. What sort of battery is it?'

Greg pulled out his mobile and showed him.

'If you like, you can leave it here. I've got the same charger and if we leave it plugged in for a bit, it'll soon charge up. I'm David, by the way.'

'That's very good of you.' Greg

handed the phone over and the other man plugged it into a socket behind his desk.

'No worries. It's a rapid charger so it won't take more than an hour. Why don't you go and find another battery in the meantime and call back for it later?'

Greg was suddenly suspicious. Why was this chap being so helpful to a stranger?

'Would you mind if I wait here? If this one's charged, I won't really need another. And besides, the message might come in while I wait.'

'Please yourself.' Did he seem less friendly, Greg wondered. 'Help yourself to water if you want it.'

The phone rang and David was busy talking to someone for the next few minutes. Was he alone in the office or was there another room?

The door opened and a couple came in. David nodded at them and gestured towards the seats.

'Morning,' said the woman. 'Hot out there, isn't it?'

'Certainly is. You live here?' Greg asked.

'Up in the mountains. It's much cooler, and more peaceful, too.'

'Mr and Mrs Halliday — nice to meet you. How can we help?' David asked as soon as the phone call was finished.

They conducted their business and Greg looked at his watch anxiously. He would wait no longer. Clearly Jeremy's office, or whatever it was, had left no message, so it was up to him to try to organise some help. As soon as David was free again, he would collect his phone and find the police station. He had wasted enough time already and Amy would be getting frantic.

The couple at the desk seemed in no hurry. He hadn't been listening to the conversation but now he tuned in again.

'I'll get you some coffee,' David was saying. 'Would you like a cup? Greg, isn't it?'

'That's kind of you but I think I'll be

on my way. If I could have my phone?'

'Leave it a bit longer. Have a coffee and then it might be finished charging. I'll check for any messages for you again in a minute.'

He went into the back room and returned a few minutes later with three cups.

'Won't be long. Now, Mrs Halliday, how's that gorgeous granddaughter of yours?'

The conversation droned on and Greg found his eyelids drooping. He'd had little sleep the previous night and the strain and exertion were getting to him.

'Nodded off already,' David was saying, as he held out the cup of coffee.

'Sorry. Must be the heat. One sugar, thanks.' He took the cup gratefully and drank it down. It was surprisingly good coffee.

'Thanks very much. That was great. Now, if you'll excuse me, I'd better get on my way.'

David unhooked the phone and

handed it back. It was almost fully charged.

'That's really good of you. Thank you very much.'

'You were going to give me the number in case your message arrives?' David said.

'It's all right. I'll look in again later. Look, I'm not sure why you're being so helpful, but I'm very grateful,' Greg said sincerely.

'I do a lot of work for several companies, people in the area. They often use me as a base for messages when they can't contact people directly. We get business out of it, one way or another.'

'I see. Well, I'll be in touch. And thanks again.' Now he had his phone in service again, he'd made his mind up to try to contact Jeremy's office again before he went to the police station.

Outside the street, he typed in the code word BUZZARD again and dialled the number, then went to sit on a seat in front of the sea and watch children playing on the beach as if nothing at all was happening in the world around. He tapped his feet impatiently. At last the phone rang.

'Who's calling?' the voice asked. Greg went through the long security rigmarole again and at last he seemed to be accepted. 'How can I help?' asked the voice.

'I've been going round the currency offices in Mojácar, trying to get the message you promised to send. Nobody's heard anything.'

'No. I'm sorry but your contact isn't in her office today.'

'It would have been nice if you'd let me know.'

'It's not easy. Besides, we didn't want to phone if you were unable to take the call for any reason.'

'Well, I'm here now. What do I do?'

'We recommend that you do nothing. In fact, we would advise you to return to England as soon as possible.'

'Don't be ridiculous! I'm not leaving without Amy and her father. If you can't offer any help, then I'll go to the local police and see what can be done myself.'

'That would be most unwise of you,' the female voice said.

'Don't patronise me,' Greg snapped. 'I'd assumed you were actually on our side. But if you have your own agenda and there's something we don't know about, then it should be your duty to make me aware of it.' There was a long pause. 'Well?' he demanded. 'Do I get some backing or am I on my own?'

'Return home. It's the only sensible thing to do,' he was told, and the connection was broken. He was truly on his own.

He put the phone in his pocket and crossed the road to where there was a large pictorial map of the town. He looked up the police station and set off to find it. It might be tricky with the language barrier, but they must have someone there who could understand him.

'Don't worry, Amy, I'm on my way,'

he muttered, with a quick glance at his watch. He could scarcely believe it was past one o'clock already.

★   ★   ★

At the police station, he found one man on duty. It was lunchtime and evidently nobody expected any crimes to be committed over the lunch period. Even worse, the desk sergeant spoke no English.

'I need help,' Greg tried. 'My friend is being held prisoner.' The man stared at him and held his hands out in a gesture of helplessness, and Greg sighed. Why had he never studied languages?

He pointed at his watch and said the word English. The man grinned and pointed to four on his own watch, and Greg hoped he'd conveyed that he was asking when someone might be there with an understanding of English. Four o'clock perhaps. That meant he had a long wait ahead. He might as well get some lunch. His next meal could be some while away.

He went out into the street again and found a café where he ordered his favourite pizza and a large bottle of water. Catching sight of himself in the mirror he was shocked to see how grubby he looked. He was unshaven, and his hair looked distinctly unkempt. No wonder people weren't taking him seriously. Maybe he should take a room somewhere and try to clean himself up a bit.

After he had eaten, it was still only three o'clock, so he decided to try to find a chemist or somewhere selling the basic toiletries and then a cheap room somewhere. If nothing else, it would help to pass the time.

He picked up the various items he needed at a small supermarket, and even bought a cheap T-shirt to allow himself the luxury of a change of clothes. Afterwards, he went to a small back street hotel and booked a room for the night. As soon as he had shaved and showered and put on the new T-shirt, he felt very much better. Leaving the carrier bag with his meagre possessions he went back to the police station. This time a younger man was on the desk.

'Do you speak English?' Greg asked hopefully.

'Certainly, sir. How can I help you?'

'I know this is going to sound very odd but I have been kept locked up at a villa just outside Las Minas. I escaped last night but my . . . my girlfriend and her father are still there. He's being forced to do some work for the owner and Amy and I came to see what was going on. We've been held there for several days now.'

The young desk sergeant stared at him and gave a smile.

'I see, sir. And your name?' Greg told him and he wrote it down. Another policeman came to the desk and when he was told in rapid Spanish what was going on, he laughed.

'Look,' Greg spluttered, 'this is serious. I'm not joking and nor is this a laughing matter.'

'You think lives are in danger and you

want us to take you to the villa and search it?'

'That's right.'

'You'd be amazed at the number of people who make similar requests. And when we arrive at the destination, they thank us for the ride.'

'You've got to take me seriously,' Greg insisted. 'I tell you, we've been held there for days. I walked practically all the way down here in the middle of the night. Now, please, if you can't act yourself, let me see someone with more influence.'

'I'm afraid our chief does not have any English.'

'Oh, come on.' Greg had never felt so frustrated. 'You have to believe me. The villa is owned by Señor Ignacio Parra-Moreno. He has a man called Juan working for him. It's him who locks us in and brings us meals.'

'We know the señor; he is a generous benefactor of our town.' The two policemen babbled away in Spanish again while Greg ground his teeth in anguish. How was he going to convince them?

'Look, I know this sounds implausible but you must believe me. They sent Amy, my friend, an air ticket and said her father was waiting for her. I came, too, to look after her. We were taken to the villa and locked in a room. Amy was allowed to see her father only briefly. He is working on some project for the señor. We were told that he would work better knowing Amy was here. Doesn't that sound like a threat to you?'

'And you were kept locked in a . . . what-do-you-say . . . an underground store and left to starve?'

'No, of course not. But we were locked in the rooms and food was brought on a tray.'

'Brought by this Juan. And you never saw the señor?'

'Well, yes. He invited us to lunch one day.'

'I see. And yet you claim to remain captive?'

Greg closed his eyes. He had to

admit, it all sounded very strange, but if the police didn't believe him, and Jeremy's office were unwilling to help, what was he going to do? He banged his fist on the counter.

'Please — we must do something.'

'Come back in the morning. We will speak to our chief and if he will authorise a search, we will go to the villa tomorrow. But I must warn you, if this is some elaborate hoax, you will suffer consequences. The señor is a well respected member of our community. Now, if you have a contact number and an address, we will be in touch.'

'There's nothing you can do today?'

'I'm sorry, sir. Now, you have a cell phone number?' Greg nodded and recited it, and the name of the hotel where he had booked in. There was nothing more he could do. In a few hours it would be dark.

He went out to find a meal, all the time his brain churning. Should he risk sending a text to Amy? What could he say? But at least she would be glad to know that he was safe, even if unable to do much.

He typed in the words: *Safe in town. Hope for police co-operation a.m. tomorrow. Love you.* xx He put in Amy's number and pressed send.

Why had he put the last thing? *Love you.* He realised he probably did love her, but was it the love of long friend-ship, or something more? He tried to convince himself the words were simply a precaution in case someone else read the message. It would be natural for a fiancé to say it, and they *were* supposed to be engaged . . .

★   ★   ★

Lying on her bed, Amy felt her silent phone give a small jolt. She went into the ensuite, assuming she wasn't being watched in there. She still hadn't located a camera in her room but she didn't want to take any risks.

As she read the message, she felt tears welling up. Greg was safe, even if

219

he couldn't bring help right away.

OK, she typed in. *Moved to new room. Dad finishing work soon. Can't wait 2 C U. Love you too. xx* As she pressed send, she wondered where he would be when he received it.

She hugged herself. He'd said he loved her! After this nightmare was over, were they really going to make it as a couple? She really hoped so.

Greatly relieved that Greg hadn't been recaptured, she went to bed and actually fell asleep quickly.

She woke the next morning as the maid brought her breakfast.

'Thank you,' she said. The maid nodded at her and hesitated, as if she was about to say something, but then her eyes drifted towards the window blind, and then she left the room, locking the door behind her.

Amy crossed to the blind and looked for some sort of listening device. There was no camera this time — but a tiny microphone was hidden at the end of the roller blind. Thank goodness she hadn't made any sound when she'd received and sent the text messages!

When would Greg get here? She ate some breakfast, wishing she didn't feel so alone. Was her father eating his breakfast? She recalled his comments from the previous night. He'd almost sounded as if he was willingly co-operating with these people. If that was really true, why had she been brought here?

★ ★ ★

As soon as he had eaten breakfast and drunk several cups of coffee, Greg went back to the police station. A different duty sergeant sat at the desk. His English was not as good as his colleague's but they did manage to communicate. He went to the back of the office and picked up several sheets of paper, read through them, and nodded at Greg.

'Please to wait,' he ordered and disappeared, only to return with two more policemen.

'Come,' one of them instructed.

They ushered him into a police car, and they drove up the steep roads to the village. They seemed to know exactly where to go. The villa gates opened magically when they sounded the horn. They drove up to the house, where they all got out in front of the imposing carved wooden doors. Juan appeared and took them inside, smiling silkily at the visitors and speaking in rapid Spanish. He showed them into a large sitting room and Greg heard the name of the señor among the flood of Spanish.

'Good day,' Ignacio Parra-Moreno said as he came into the room. 'You are English, I understand.'

Greg stared at him. 'You know I am.' What game was this? The señor was acting as if they had never met before. 'You entertained me . . . us . . . Amy and me, to lunch the other day. With wine from your vineyards.'

'I'm sorry, you are mistaken. I have never met you before.'

The policemen spoke in rapid Spanish, and he gave a gracious bow. Evidently they had asked to search the house and he had agreed.

'Where is it you allege that you were held prisoner here?'

'In a room on the lower floor. There are two rooms and a bathroom between them. And surveillance cameras hidden in the lights.'

The señor laughed aloud at the words. 'But such a place does not exist! There are several guest rooms, but that is all. You are free to look.'

They all trooped out and walked along the several corridors to the oak door with its bolts. Greg motioned towards it.

'Through there. Down some stairs and there are the two rooms.'

The door was unbolted by the smirking Juan and everyone descended.

The rooms which had become so familiar to Greg had been completely changed. Instead of the beds and desks, the whole place was stacked with old furniture.

'But I don't understand.' He opened

the door to the bathroom. At least that was as he remembered it. 'This is where we were kept.'

'This was once a guest suite, but as you can see, it hasn't been used for some time.' While the señor repeated his words in Spanish for the benefit of the police, Greg stood under the light and peered up at it, looking for evidence of the camera, but it, too, had gone. The second room was much the same as the first.

He remembered Amy's text.

'Amy said she's been moved to another room. Perhaps we can look elsewhere? And the building in the garden where her father is working — perhaps you will allow us to see that?'

'I am afraid not. Mr Poolley's work is confidential. But you may see him, if he can spare the time.'

Greg could hardly believe this. Surely Jeremy would never co-operate with these men? Not unless Amy was under threat?

'What makes you think this Amy's room has been changed? Whoever Amy is,' the señor asked him.

'My fiancée, as you well know. Jeremy's daughter.'

'This is ludicrous.' The señor spoke again to the policemen who were by now looking quite uncomfortable.

'Let us see Mr Poolley, then,' Greg said desperately.

The señor shrugged and led them all back up the stairs, through the lounge and out on to the terrace.

'See if Mr Poolley can spare the time to come out here,' he said to Juan, and Greg began to feel suspicious once more. The feeling that he was about to be made a fool of persisted, and he still hadn't seen any sign of Amy, wherever she was.

He watched and waited. The others were chatting in their own language and he could see that the conversation was cordial.

'Excuse me,' the señor said. 'You do not speak Spanish?' Greg shook his

225

head. 'I was offering refreshments before your journey back to town.'

Pressing the button on an intercom, he ordered something, and moments later the maid arrived with a tray of coffee and pastries.

Greg smiled at her. 'Hello again. You remember me, don't you?'

She stared at him and then at the señor before turning to leave the room, clearly under orders to make no sign of recognition.

Greg was given a cup of coffee and added sugar and milk, but he declined the pastries.

In time he heard footsteps and saw Jeremy for the first time in several months. He couldn't get over how much he seemed to have aged.

'Uncle Jeremy,' he said uncertainly, holding out a hand.

'Greg! What on earth are you doing here? This is a surprise. When Juan said there was a visitor from England, you're the last person I was expecting. Come here, my boy.' Jeremy pulled him into a hug and patted his back. 'How are your parents? Well, I hope.'

'They were when I last saw them. A bit worried about you, though.'

'No reason to be, they know I go away rather a lot these days. But how did you get here? More to the point, how did you know I was here?'

'This is ridiculous. A charade.' Greg turned to the señor. 'What hold do you have over him? Why is he behaving like this? Where's Amy?'

'I told you — I do not know this Amy you speak of,' the señor said. 'Now, if you have quite finished, I need to return to my own work.'

'Don't give me that! She sent me a text message only last night — said she had been moved to another room here.' Juan and the señor exchanged glances and Greg knew that he shouldn't have revealed anything about the text. Now their mobile phones would be searched for and confiscated. He needed to send her another text, to warn her.

'I need a bathroom,' he said abruptly.

He was shown to a small room at one side of the hallway and prayed he would get a signal there. He ran the tap and quickly wrote a message: *Am at house but not believed. They know you have phone. Hide it. Will be back later. J cooperating with them. G.*

As he had feared, there was no signal, so he left it un-sent, ready to press the button as soon as possible. He flushed the toilet and went outside to where Juan was waiting for him.

'What's the game?' he asked.

'No game. We're just cleverer people than you are.'

'Where's Amy? If you've hurt her, I'll . . . I'll . . . '

'Bring the police back here?' he said with a smirk.

They returned to the lounge where the atmosphere was relaxed with everyone smiling and joking.

'Now, if you have seen everything you need, I have work to do,' the señor said.

'And I shall return to my work,' Jeremy said, also smiling. 'It's great to see you again, Greg. Enjoy your stay, and give my regards to your parents when you get back to England. Oh, and congratulations on your engagement to my daughter. I couldn't be more delighted.' He shook Greg's hand, holding it tightly for several seconds.

'Thank you, Jeremy. It's good of you to say so.'

As the older man left the room, the police thanked the señor for his co-operation and they left the house. While everyone was thus distracted, Greg pressed the send button on his phone, deep in his pocket, and hoped he was in time.

* * *

'We may be making charges against you,' he was told by the English speaking officer at the police station, 'for wasting our time, and the señor may choose to make a complaint against you.'

'I'll get to the bottom of this

somehow,' Greg said. 'You know where to find me.' He left the station with no clear idea of what to do next.

He might as well check out of his hotel, he decided; there was no point in keeping on his room when he wouldn't be using it. It wasn't as if he had any luggage — a supermarket carrier bag contained his worldly possessions at this time. He paid the few euros owing and walked back towards the sea front, feeling certain that Amy was still at the villa. If she had left, she would have got a message to him somehow.

He sat in a café and drank a cold beer, willing a message to appear on his phone and trying to plan what he would do next. He had a deep foreboding about Jeremy's compliance with the men holding him and wished he'd had the opportunity to speak to him privately.

His mobile rang. It was an unknown number.

'Is that Greg?'

'Yes.'

'It's David. From Currency Exchange. You were expecting a message? It's arrived. If you'd like to call in at the office, I can let you have it.'

'Really? Thank you very much. I'll be right there.'

That was strange. How had David got his number? He felt certain he hadn't given it to him. They had talked about it but he was sure the conversation had turned to his low battery before he'd actually given it. Perhaps he had noted it while he had been charging the battery.

It was very peculiar. The person he had last spoken to at Jeremy's office had been adamant that he should return home, but they must know that he hadn't followed their advice.

He walked through the quiet back streets, passing a small sitting area en route with a sign: *Avenida Parra-Moreno*. Clearly this was why the man was so well respected in the town.

He arrived at the currency office hoping this wasn't some sort of trap.

David was behind his desk. 'Oh, hi,' he said in a friendly manner. 'This arrived late last night. Sorry I didn't get in touch before.' He handed Greg a sealed enveloped.

'Thanks. How was it delivered?'

'It was a fax. I put it in an envelope for you in case anyone else found it lying around.'

'I see. Thanks. How did you get my phone number, by the way?'

'You gave it to me,' David said immediately.

'I don't think I did.'

'Really? I can't explain it then. Anyhow, I hope that's the news you were waiting for. Is there anything else? Another charge for your mobile phone battery, perhaps?'

'Thanks, but no. I appreciate your help though.'

'No problem. We always try to help our English friends.'

Greg opened the envelope outside, a foolish gesture, he realised, since David must have read the message before sealing it in the envelope.

Booking reference for flight: 1800 hours, Murcia. XJ316. Meet representative in airport lounge for further clarification.

Clearly someone had booked a flight home for him and ignored everything he had said about making sure Amy and Jeremy were safe. Well, there was no way he was going anywhere without the others.

He stuffed the page into his pocket and continued on his way, musing that there was something else going on that he didn't understand. Maybe he *should* go home. But how could he even think of it until he had Amy with him? And Jeremy, too, if possible. Besides, he realised, there was no date given for this flight — it could mean any time in the next few days. And what sort of representative was he supposed to meet? Representative of what? Everything was becoming an endless stream of questions to which there were no answers.

What to do next? Perhaps David could help him find a hire car? This seemed to be the most urgent thing he needed. But could he trust David? He knew he had somehow copied his number from his phone. Quite when or why, he couldn't tell. He went back to the currency office.

'Hello again,' Greg said in as friendly a manner as he could muster. 'I need to hire a car for a few days. Can you suggest anywhere?'

'Certainly. One of the main dealers has an office in the town. You can leave it at the airport when you've finished.' He had a wall map of the town and pointed out the hire firm. It was quite a distance away. 'If you can wait half an hour till my lunch break, I'll drive you over there.'

'That's good of you. You always seem to be coming to my rescue.'

'No problem.'

Greg wandered down the road a little way and looked in at the shop windows, his mind racing around the possibilities and what he was going to do once he had a car to use. Going back to the villa didn't seem like a sensible option but he had to get Amy out somehow.

He found a shop selling road maps of the area and bought one, plus a specialist map showing details of the mine workings at various sites. It could be useful, he thought. He added a powerful torch to his purchases and, on impulse, a combination tool that had screwdrivers, pliers and other attachments. He smiled wryly. A boys' toy, he thought. But it might be useful.

Escape!

Amy sat in her room, trying to read. There were several books to choose from, mostly novels, but she found it impossible to concentrate, listening as she was for the sound of cars coming up the hill. She even packed all her things into her rucksack, ready for a quick getaway when Greg arrived. She hoped her father would also be able to make a quick getaway.

She could see little from her window except the opposite mountains. It was a spectacular sight, but it wasn't the view she wanted.

She stayed as quiet as she could, hoping she wouldn't miss anything, and did hear some footsteps at one point, but nothing more happened. She also heard the rattle of cups and saucers and, later, doors closing. She thought of shouting out but doubted it would be worth the effort.

It must have been approaching lunch-time when her mobile vibrated. She went into the ensuite again and looked at the text message from Greg, warning her to hide her phone.

How was she supposed to do that? She'd thought it was already in the safest place, tucked in her trousers, but they might insist on searching her.

Frowning, she looked around the room. She had some sticking plaster in her toilet kit; she might be able to use it to stick it inside a drawer or under the desk. It was a very tiny phone, luckily.

She pulled off the backing from several of the plasters and used them to attach her phone to the underside of the bedside cupboard.

She had just managed to flush the pieces of backing down the toilet when the door opened. It was Juan and the maid. He instructed the girl to search Amy's pockets and to pat her down each leg to make sure the missing phone wasn't hidden about her. Thank heavens for Greg's warning.

'What in earth are you doing?' Amy protested indignantly.

The maid shook her head at Juan, who then proceeded to tip out all her things from the rucksack and her toilet bag. He pulled the bedcovers off and even tossed the mattress to one side.

'Where is it?' he snarled.

'I don't know what you're talking about.'

'We know you have a cell phone somewhere. Your boyfriend told us. Oh, yes, did you know he's been here looking for you? The police were highly amused. Even your father was surprised by the intrusion.'

'Is he all right? My father, I mean?'

'Of course. He's looking forward to his generous reward when the work is complete. He will be a rich man.'

'I don't know what you're talking about,' Amy said, slightly uncertain.

'Your father has co-operated well. He will have his reward for his part in the work which will make us all wealthy. So

I advise you to co-operate with us as your father has done. Now, where is your cell phone?'

'You took our phone when we first arrived, remember? There is no other one. Perhaps Greg bought one when he escaped.'

'He is leaving the country on a flight this evening. He has his booking already, so I suggest you forget him and stop being so uncooperative.'

Amy ignored him and began to set her bed to rights and re-pack her bag, while Juan was still moving round the room, inspecting every inch of it that he could. He gestured to the maid to leave, following her out of the room, but Amy's sigh of relief was very short-lived as Juan returned.

'The señor wishes you to eat with him.'

'To give you the chance to search through my things again, no doubt,' she said, and his smirk proved she had hit the mark. 'There's nothing for you to find. You took away everything useful when we first arrived.'

She went along the corridor, almost herded forward by the unpleasant little man. Pity, she thought — she could have returned the phone to its secret pocket. She wondered what was going to happen next.

To Amy's surprise, her father was already seated at the dining-table when she arrived, looking very much at ease. She frowned, puzzled. He really did seem to be working with the Spaniard, which was not the impression she had gained at first. The two men rose as she approached.

'I am glad you were able to join us,' the señor said graciously.

'So am I. I don't like eating alone. I don't like *being* on my own.'

'It's a pity your fiancé found it necessary to leave. But he has returned to his home today so we will not be troubled by him again. I expect Juan told you of the little inconvenience we experienced this morning?'

'Is everything all right, Dad?' she

asked, ignoring the señor's pleasantries.

'It's fine, darling, truly. Señor Parra-Moreno has made us a generous offer. The work is all but finished and we shall be able to return home very soon. Once it's marketed, we shall gain a considerable amount of money, enough to be comfortable for many years to come.'

'I don't understand — why are you working with them like this? For money? I can't pretend to like the way we've been treated and threatened.'

'My sincere apologies to you, Amy. I may call you Amy?' the Spaniard said smoothly. 'There was never any threat intended, but your arrival here with a young man was unexpected and our actions became necessary. Now, please eat. And please let me pour you some wine.'

'Are you going to tell me about this work you've been doing, Dad? What's so secret about it all?'

The two men exchanged glances and the señor nodded his agreement.

'The señor has made a discovery which could influence the future for many people around the world. One of the major problems affecting the more affluent Western societies is obesity, but there are rare herbs growing mainly in quite inaccessible places which we have discovered can affect the way humans metabolise food. It is something that will make our fortunes. Something that people have wanted for many years.'

'I see. And you propose commercial production of this miracle cure?'

'Indeed. The competition for the formula will be immense. The richest people in the world will be willing to pay a fortune for the chance to eat as much as they want without putting on weight.'

'Very commendable,' Amy said bitterly. 'And what about the poverty and the hunger of the rest of the world? Might it not be better to try to find ways of solving the problems of starvation? And where is this herb grown? No, don't tell me, in the South

American rain forests. Among the starving millions who live there. Some irony, don't you think?'

'We shall be able to help them. We'll reward them with money to develop new income streams,' the señor told them. 'But we hope the work your father has been doing might enable us to synthesise the ingredients so that nobody is going to be disadvantaged.'

'And how do you get hold of this herb?'

'We have our people out there, harvesting it,' the señor told her.

'And what of the people who *were* using it for medicinal purposes?'

'They now receive money instead, to buy whatever they need.'

'Oh, I see. I bet you pay them next to nothing and they have to work like crazy for your benefit.'

'Come on, darling, this isn't the time for your campaigning. It is indeed a very rare herb, which is why I'm trying to manufacture it.'

'I don't understand. What do you

know about such things, Dad? I thought you worked for the Government.'

'Not for many years. I've been working for various industries.'

'So what was all that rubbish I had to go through to speak to someone from your office? Code words and questions — all very hush hush.'

'That's nothing for you to worry about.' He gave her a warning glance that was clearly meant to keep her quiet. 'It was probably just my secretary playing a bit of a game with you.'

'I see. Very convincing.' She decided to say nothing more that may be considered controversial but her mind was racing. She didn't believe any of this. Maybe there was some miracle slimming cure, but she found it hard to think it was the reason for all this mystery and sinister goings on. For now, though, she had to accept what her father was telling her, however implausible it sounded. She really hoped that the poor tribespeople weren't being exploited, but she just knew they were. How could he go along with all this? Where were his once high standards?

★ ★ ★

'I still don't understand why you're helping me this way,' Greg said to David as they drove across town.

'Haven't you noticed how fellow Brits talk to each other when they're in a foreign country? They'd ignore each other at home, but when abroad, anyone speaking the same language is like a long-lost friend.'

'I'm grateful to you but I'm not sure I can believe you.'

'Never mind, just accept it. It breaks the boredom for me. So, where have you been staying since you arrived?'

'Several places really.' He named the hotel where they'd spent the first night and the place he'd stayed the previous night. 'I also went up to the mountains and stayed in a village there.'

'Yes, Las Minas. These things get around. We know most English speakers hereabouts. Several of them have homes up in the mountains, especially around Las Minas. It's very picturesque.'

'But how did you know I was staying there?'

'I didn't, it was a lucky guess. Now, it's just along here. Are you catching that flight tonight? If so, you only need a special one-day rental.'

'I doubt I'll make that flight. So you did read my fax?' Greg commented.

David stopped the car outside the car rental agency.

'Of course. It's useful to have whatever knowledge you can come by.'

'So why was your office the one to get my message? You're working for Señor Parra-Moreno, aren't you?'

'Let's just say I have friends all around the world and the señor is among them. He's very generous. We have a good international set-up and . . . well, we like to help whenever possible. Mention my name in there and they'll give you a discount. Off you go now. And good luck.'

Greg climbed out of the car and quickly David drove away.

Greg felt even more perplexed, but that was becoming his normal state these days. David had evidently been instructed to help him and was probably supposed to ensure that he did leave on this flight.

A few minutes later, Greg was driving away in a small saloon car, much like the one his mother drove at home. He frowned. He really must send them a message to let them know he was all right. Problem was, he wasn't sure that Amy and Jeremy *were* all right.

With no definite plans, he drove back towards the little mountain village. It looked very beautiful and peaceful in the sunshine. He saw the road that led up to the villa and drove past it, wondering if there were any other routes around the area. Espying a rather rough track leading higher up the mountain, he followed it, hoping the suspension on the little car would hold out. However, as he drew closer to it, he quailed at the sight of the track — it was almost vertical. Still, with no alternative but to continue he started up, though when he reached a wider place he stopped the car to check his map and glance across to the other side of the valley.

The village was already way below him and Mojácar a mere white haze in the distance. He wished he had some binoculars to get a close-up of the villa across the valley.

There was a steep drop between him and the lovely house but he could at least see a bit more of the layout. He could see the swimming pool glinting bright blue and the wide red roof stretching over the many rooms. Dark shrubs and palms grew all around the house and he thought of the shady garden, what little they had been able to see of it.

As he stared, he was certain he could see Amy and her father walking together. They went inside the little building where Mr Poolley had been doing his work. The shadows were lengthening as the sun dipped behind the mountains. Greg wasn't sure it was a good idea to remain out there for the night, and he didn't fancy driving down that steep road in the dark. Perhaps he would go into the village and see if there was somewhere he might stay for the night.

As he drove down the scarily steep slope he was aware of numerous openings in the rocks. Many looked man-made and he assumed they were the old mine workings. He stopped near to one of them, parking carefully to one side, and took out the mine map to trace the routes of the openings into the mountainside.

They hadn't been worked for many years, but the tunnels went for miles. That gave him an idea. Suppose there were tunnels near to the villa? Maybe he could find some route to inside the walls.

He studied the maps carefully and eventually thought he might have found something. There was nothing to say it was a clear route all the way, but there did seem to be a tunnel very close. It was worth a try at least.

He drove through the village and out to the other side, took the track leading to the villa, and looked for somewhere to park. A parked car might arouse suspicion, so it needed to be well hidden.

There was a clump of palms to one side and a narrow track leading round, so he risked the poor car's suspension once more and drove along it. He managed to park beneath the palms. Unless someone was actually looking for it, he seemed well enough screened from view.

It was dusk now and very shortly it would be full darkness. He sat back in the car and studied his map by torchlight.

He could hear the sounds of night creatures, and when an owl or some other night bird made a loud cry, it made him jump. He took a deep breath; he must try to steady his rising nervous tension.

He worked out that there was a tunnel a little higher up the track from him, and if the map was accurate, it should actually lead him into the villa's grounds. Feeling optimistic, he folded the map and tucked it into his trousers, and put the torch in his pocket. Once his eyes were used to the dark, he would be able to see where he was going. The moon was still bright and lit the path quite well. 'I'm on my way, Amy,' he murmured.

★　★　★

Amy had to swallow her disappointment at Greg's failure to convince the police of their plight, but it seemed to have one benefit, for when lunch was over, she wasn't forced back to her room but instead was allowed to wander round the gardens, though perhaps that was because her father was now fully compliant with their wishes.

She felt disappointed. He seemed to have forsaken his once strong principles and was giving in to a more mercenary frame of mind. She wondered about his other work. If he wasn't working for the Government, who exactly *was* he working for? And all that rigmarole of security at his office or whatever it was, certainly hadn't been someone playing a game. He must have been trying to stop her from saying too much.

She decided to tackle him again and went to his work room.

'Hi, Dad. Mind if I join you?'

'I'm quite busy, love. I see you're enjoying the garden. Wonderful, isn't it? It's amazing to get so much growth in this dry climate. I think they have some sort of reservoir to irrigate the land.' His eyes swept upwards to where a camera must be hidden and she picked up it.

'I was wondering if anyone would mind if I had a swim, only I'm not sure who to ask,' she said.

'I shouldn't think anyone will mind. I'd be tempted, too, if I wasn't so busy.'

Amy was looking around. Jeremy was working at a computer which had been tucked away in a cupboard when she was last in the room.

'Do you have the Internet?' she asked.

'I don't really need it. All the information I needed was presented to me. There's no telephone here anyway.' She nodded. That made more sense. 'Now, if you'll excuse me, I need to finish this segment.'

She looked at his screen. It was covered in a series of small coloured circles, all linked together with lines and squiggles. She watched for a moment as he manipulated them and they all moved around.

'Very pretty,' she murmured. He smiled and waved a hand absently.

He was behaving just as she'd always known him to. When she was a child, he'd used that same gesture to make her go away.

She went back to her room to change for her swim, hoping she wasn't tempting fate to get herself locked in again. Before she left the room she felt for the phone in its hiding place. It was still there. She was tempted to take it with her and try to find a spot to use it, but decided against it; she had nowhere to hide it if she was caught.

The swimming pool was a delight and she struck out, thinking how much Greg would have loved it. He had been away for almost two days now and she really missed him. They had never spent so much time together before, not since they were small children, but now it was different. He was everything she could want, though she worried slightly that it was the peculiar circumstances that had brought them so close together. Would they feel the same when they returned to normal life?

She lay on her back, floating in the water and wondering what he was doing now. She had half expected him to come back at any moment, but perhaps he really had returned home, as Juan had said. Yet she was certain he wouldn't have left them there without resolving anything.

She climbed up the pool steps and lay on one of the sun-beds for a few minutes to dry off, but she soon felt restless and went back to her room to get dressed.

Pulling the phone from its hiding place she took it into the ensuite and switched it on. There was no message from Greg and she wondered about sending him one. But what could she say? So she turned it off again, deciding to conserve the battery for when she might need it.

She took a shower to wash away the chlorine, then put on her only clean shirt and a skirt and lay back on her bed to relax, but when she realised the door was still unlocked she hid the phone again and went back into the garden.

Because they were high up the mountainside, the sun seemed to disappear quite quickly and the garden was in shadow. Her father came out of his room to join her.

'Shall we take a stroll?' he suggested. They linked arms and wandered among the trees and shrubs.

'How far do the grounds stretch?' she asked.

'Several acres. There's a wall round most of it and a security fence.'

'To keep us in or other people out?'

'Bit of both, I suppose. Security is quite an issue around these parts.'

They reached a steep slope where the rocks were quite loose. Amy saw a dark patch ahead and went towards it.

'There's some sort of cave down there,' she indicated.

'The place is riddled with them. Old mine workings, I suppose.'

As they turned back towards the house, Amy commented, 'I wonder why the police didn't believe Greg this morning? Probably because they believe the señor rather than the Brits. How did Greg seem?'

'Fine. A bit puzzled. He's turned into a fine young man, by the way. Do you think there really is a future for you?'

'I hope so. Dad, can I ask about this work of yours? It isn't like you. I've always admired your complete integrity.'

'The world we live in today has changed. It's swim with the sharks or drown, I'm afraid, and I'm choosing the former. Now, shall we go and see if they've brought us any supper?'

They turned back and went to his room, unaware that Greg had been watching from the mountainside across the valley.

A tray of the ubiquitous cold meats and salad was waiting for them, with some fresh bread, a flask of wine and a bowl of fruit. There was also a vacuum pot holding hot soup. They sat at the little table and ate in silence. Being watched was not conducive to conversation.

'Is there a Mrs Señor?' she asked.

'I think so. She's away, though. I

think she's in some sort of clinic having treatment, but I may be wrong.'

'For obesity perhaps. Maybe that's why he's so interested in finding this so-called cure.' She yawned. 'Oh dear — too much wine, I suppose. I might go to bed now.'

'I'll spend a bit more time on the computer and then I'll turn in, too. See you in the morning.'

She gave him a hug. However much she disapproved of what he was doing, he was still her beloved father.

'Trust me,' he breathed in her ear.

It was hot and stuffy in her room. She undressed and then, for some reason she couldn't explain, pulled on her coolest trousers. She had the feeling that she should always be ready in case she needed to move quickly. In the dark, she took out her phone again and switched it on. There was still no message. Perhaps Greg didn't want to give anything away in case they had taken her phone away. That must be it.

She typed in a message to let him

know she still had the phone, typed *OK* so that he knew she was safe, and added *Love you* before sending it.

She waited for a few minutes in case he sent a message back, but then switched it off and hid it again before lying back on the bed, listening to the night sounds, and wishing Greg was her with her.

★ ★ ★

Greg was just entering the dark opening to either a cave or a mine shaft when his mobile beeped. He read the message from Amy and smiled. Good girl! She had managed to hide her phone. He considered replying but decided against it. He didn't know how successful this latest plan was going to be and he didn't want to raise her hopes.

He was longing to see her again and knew that when he did, he wanted to hold her in his arms and never let her go. Funny, after all these years. He'd never thought of her in any romantic way before, but this last week, despite their experiences, he knew there was now something much more.

Still, all this musing wasn't getting him anywhere . . .

He gritted his teeth and went into the black opening, shining the torch around. The wide opening soon narrowed and he walked along gingerly, taking care not to lose his footing. The floor dipped down and he was travelling downhill for a distance. That wasn't right, he thought; he had expected a fairly steep climb upwards, not down.

He retraced his steps to the entrance and shone the torch round the small cavern, and spotted another passage leading in a different direction.

This time he really was climbing up, but it was very hot inside and the air was stale, not a good omen — it might mean there was no exit at the other end and no through draught. But he had no alternative but to continue. He tried to estimate how much farther up the mountain he would have travelled to reach the villa by road — probably at least half a kilometre. In a dark tunnel, it would seem much farther.

As he came to a wider space and shone the torch round to see which way he should go, it appeared to be a dead end. He couldn't believe it. After all the effort, to meet with a blank was so disappointing. There *must* be a route here! He shone the torch upwards . . . and saw an opening way above him. But how did he get up there? And if he *did* rescue Amy and Jeremy, how would they get down?

He walked round the edge of the cave and found the remains of an old ladder. Evidently that was how he should get up to the tunnel entrance.

He tried it against the wall. It was dangerous in the extreme, but once he climbed up, he thought he could improvise a way down if necessary. There might even be some rope somewhere. He tested each rung before putting his weight on it and slowly, despite many missing pieces, he got closer and closer to the opening. He was panting hard and dripping with sweat by the time he reached the top. His hands were damp, making his grip even more tenuous, but he had made it.

After a short rest, he set off again. This tunnel was much narrower, more as if it was just a passage than where rocks or minerals had been removed. A sudden draught reached him, a welcome breath of fresh air, and he breathed it in gratefully. The torch showed a grating ahead, and bushes growing. Was it possible that he was in the grounds of the villa?

Greg pushed at the grating but it was held firmly in place. It wouldn't budge. But he was not going to be defeated at this stage.

He poked around the rocks at the edge of the grille, and noticing that one of the bars was rusty, he worked at it with his pocket knife until it broke off. With the iron bar, he dug away at the edges and gradually loosened the rocks. As they finally gave way and rattled off down the slope, he hoped that the dogs he'd heard before were safely under control.

At last he stepped out and looked around him. He was clearly in the garden. 'Thank heavens,' he breathed.

He was a long way down the garden on the rough mountainside, and could see the fence stretching out below him. He realised he needed a marker in case he had to find the tunnel to make a swift exit.

He still had some pieces of the survival blanket in his pocket; he would hang a piece of the silvery foil on a bush nearby. It would only be seen if the torch light caught it.

Approaching the villa, he saw that the windows of the rooms where they had been kept were in darkness, and remembered that Amy had been moved. He had no idea where she was now. He would have to risk another text message.

Where R U? I'm outside. Put light on. G.

Nothing happened. He looked at his watch. It was almost midnight. Please don't be asleep, Amy. Check your phone! But his telepathic messages were having no effect. Should he try waking Jeremy?

As silently as he could, Greg walked round the garden, hoping to see some clue that might lead him to Amy. He was cautious, knowing that there were sensors which might alert anyone to his presence.

Seeing nothing, in desperation he dialled Amy's number. It rang without answer. Had it been taken off her? But having got this far, he wasn't about to give up. He tried to remember where the alarm had gone off on his previous wanderings, thinking he could throw a stone at it and make enough noise to rouse Amy. But even as he was wondering about the wisdom of this, his own phone rang, almost making him jump out of his skin. He answered it immediately.

'Greg? I've put my light on. I'm

being overheard but if you're quick, we might make it.'

'Can't see it. Are you locked in?'

'I don't think so.'

'OK. Put on trainers and trousers, leave everything behind, and come down past the swimming pool. I'll wait in the bushes.'

He sat still, his heart racing. He wasn't sure what they would do but getting Amy back by his side was all he could think of at present.

He heard a creak and thought it might be the door. Peering through the darkness he saw her coming and flicked his torch on and off. She sank to the ground beside him and he pulled her into his arms.

'Oh, thanks heavens!' He held her tight. 'Gosh, I've missed you.'

'It's so good to see you too,' she murmured. 'What's the plan?'

'There's an old mine tunnel down at the bottom of the garden. It's a bit tricky and slippery, but if you're willing to give it a go . . . ?'

'Of course. Then what?'

'I've got a hire care parked near the entrance. But what about your father? Can we get him out?'

'I think we should make our escape, quite honestly. I don't think he's in danger now. Things seem to have changed. I'll tell you about it later.'

'Have you seen any rope lying around?' Greg asked, remembering the steep drop that lay ahead of them.

'There are some lifebelts by the pool. They're on ropes. Why?'

'I'll grab some. Wait here.' He shot off into the darkness and she heard scuffling noises. What on earth was he doing?

After what seemed like an age, he came back with a couple of lengths.

'OK. Come on now — move quietly.'

They slithered down the steep slope and reached the lower level.

'It's near here somewhere . . . ' Suddenly lights flashed on all round the villa and they heard the dogs barking.

'Oh no,' Greg muttered. He flashed

the torch on again and saw his metal foil strip shining in the light. 'Quick, down here!'

They hurtled down the last few yards and he snatched the foil as he passed it.

'Follow me!' He squeezed through the narrow gap, dragging Amy after him, then shoved the grille back. They sat panting in the dark, clutching hands. The dogs, fortunately held on leads, passed quite close by but somehow didn't sense them and moved on.

When all was silent again, Greg spoke softly.

'Are you sure about leaving your father? What's been happening?'

'I think he's actually working for the señor quite happily. They were talking about money. Enough for an easy life, was the implication. I suspect Dad's sold his soul and all that. I hope not but . . . Anyway, they seemed to think the work would be complete in a few days and that he would be free to go home after that. He was talking about us having a holiday, just as if nothing had happened.'

'And you weren't locked in any more?'

'Not after the police came this morning. I was invited to join the señor and Dad for lunch and then left to wander. I even had a swim.'

'Lucky you! The police were threatening to bring charges against me for wasting their time. There are several places with Parra-Moreno written on them in town — a park thing and a road. He's clearly big in Mojácar. Are you OK now? Shall we go?'

They set off down the dark tunnel. For some of the way they walked side by side, holding hands; on the narrow bits, Greg walked behind her, shining the torch ahead so they could see the ground.

'So why do we need rope?' Amy asked suddenly.

'Ah, yes. Well, there's a very steep bit. I scrambled up on an old ladder which is practically disintegrating. I didn't think we should risk it for the downward journey. I'm not entirely certain we'll manage it even with the rope, but at least it may help. Steady now, we're nearly there. I'll see if I can fix the rope to something and then we'll give it a go.'

Amazingly there were some old metal fixings in the rock face. The miners must have used them for some sort of hoist.

'This doesn't look too strong but it should hold our weights. Do you want to go first?' Greg offered.

'No, you go,' Amy said. 'Then if I slip you'll break my fall.'

Greg laughed. 'OK, here I go.'

He grasped the rope, then, tucking it under his legs to use as a break if he needed it, began to walk down the wall, letting it out as he went. Amy shone the light on him, feeling terrified at what lay ahead of her.

'Darn it!' came Greg's voice from below. 'It's six feet short. I'll have to drop the last bit. Don't worry — I can catch you when you come down.'

She heard a thump as he landed and a groan.

'What's happened?' she demanded.

'Nothing, it's all right. I just bashed my foot on a rock. You ready? Send the torch down first.' She did so and he shone it up to her.

Trembling, she wrapped the rope around herself as Greg had done and set off down the wall of rock. He shone the light up and watched as she clumsily jerked her way down until at last her feet were just above him.

'OK. When you feel me touching your feet, let go and I'll let you down.'

They both ended in a heap on the ground but they had made it.

His foot hurt when he stood up, but somehow they continued along to the entrance. The torch battery was all but gone as they emerged into the moonlight.

'The car's just a bit further on. I'm not sure what we should do next. They must have discovered you're missing so they'll probably send someone out to look for us. We could sit tight till it's light, or we could risk going down now. What do you think?'

'I'd really like to get away from this place. But if you think it might be safer to stay here, that's what we'll do. You can tell me everything that's been happening to you. What were the police really like?'

So, they sat tight and talked for a few hours, bringing each other up to date with everything. When they saw the sky turning pink with the new dawn, they decided to move.

'We could just drive to the airport and go home,' Greg suggested.

'We can't. I left my passport in my rucksack.'

'And you've no other identity papers?'

She shook her head. 'Nor money nor tickets or anything. I was so intent on getting away, I never even thought.'

'That's a bit of a blow, but then, I did say to leave everything. Never mind, we'll think of something. Let's get down to the town and decide on our next move. There's still all my stuff at the villa, too. Not that it really matters but I was quite fond of that old rucksack. We've shared a lot.'

He was silent for a while as he thought through the options.

'Do you think the police would believe me if we went back together to retrieve our belongings?' Amy suggested.

'If our things are still there . . . Do you know, they'd piled old furniture in our rooms and made them look like an old cellar or something? They denied we'd ever been there. Mind you, the maid looked a bit sympathetic. Maybe she would vouch for us.'

'What happened about the buzzard connection?'

'Nothing. They just sent me a flight number and said someone would meet me at the airport, and told me to go home. That was yesterday.'

'Maybe we should try them again?'

'We might ask that David character.

He works for the currency place. He seemed helpful — unusually so.'

'Can we trust him?'

Greg shrugged. 'Pass. He admitted to doing odd jobs for Ignacio. I suspect he's just a bit of an opportunist. But he's the only contact we have here, and he might be able to give us some advice at least.'

★　★　★

They arrived in the town almost before anywhere was open. Predictably Greg was famished and wanted breakfast as his first priority.

'It's all right for you,' he moaned. 'You've been well fed for the last two days. I've been living on crisps and bottles of water.'

They found a café that was just opening. Greg was delighted to discover that they provided English breakfasts as their speciality.

'We'll have two, please. And lots of coffee. And cereal to start.'

Once he was refuelled, having eaten his own and most of Amy's breakfast, too, Greg left some money on the table and stood up.

'Shall we see if the currency place is open? Or shall we try the buzzard thing again?'

'Buzzard, I'd say. Then if they point us back at the currency place, we'll know we can trust him.'

Greg typed in the word and sent it. He waited for a few minutes and then his phone rang. He handed it to Amy. She went through the security procedure and then explained the situation.

'So my passport is still at the villa and all our things, although Greg has some money and credit cards. We had to escape in the night and I didn't bring anything with me.'

'I see,' said the woman. 'Tricky. Let me see what I can do and I'll get back to you. On this same number?'

'Yes, please. My battery's flat.'

They strolled along the sea front holding hands, but it didn't seem right to speak of their feelings until the other matters were resolved.

'Did you find out why your father made a new will?' Greg queried.

'I didn't ask, but knowing how long solicitors take to do anything, it must have been planned weeks ago. I wonder if we'll ever be back to normal?'

'Whatever normal is. But, Amy, whatever happens, I really hope . . . ' He stopped as his phone rang. 'Your friends,' he said, handing it over.

'Amy. We feel the only thing possible is to go to the villa again and demand that your possessions are restored to you. If the police are no help, then take an independent witness with you. We suggest David from the currency exchange. We have worked with him before and he's pretty reliable. Take some pictures of yourselves at the villa and send them to us. Just as a precaution. I assume your phone can do this?'

'Yes. But what if they won't let us go once we're back there?'

'That's unlikely if David is with you and his office knows where he is.'

'He certainly gets around. He works for the señor, too.'

'Don't worry about that. He's just conveniently on the ground there.'

'OK, but the people at the villa denied we were ever there when Greg took the police yesterday. They'd stored a load of stuff in our rooms and the police clearly believed the señor rather than Greg or even my father.'

'But you need to get your possessions, so at least give it a try. We'll arrange a flight home for you once we know you have your things.'

'And Dad? What about him?'

'We'll inform you of progress on that when appropriate.' Amy told Greg of the plans.

'OK, so let's go to the office and see if David will come with us.'

The Truth At Last

An hour later, they were once more driving up to the Villa Parra-Moreno, this time in David's car after a very hasty explanation.

'I'm not sure how we'll get in. There's some sort of video link to the house and they open the gates by remote control,' Greg told him.

They stopped outside and David sounded the horn. When nothing happened, Greg got out to see if there was a bell or buzzer. It was only as he turned back to the car that he noticed their two bags lying to one side of the gate. He nudged them with his toe, then he bent to pick them up, satisfied that all was well.

'Would you believe it?' he said when he took them back to the car. 'It's almost as if they knew we were coming. Here — check to see everything's there.'

Amy rummaged around. 'It looks like it. My passport's there, which is the most important thing, and even the hundred euro note they sent me.'

'So, back to town, I assume?' David asked.

'We'll just take a couple of pictures if that's all right. Could you take one of the two of us outside the gates?'

They made sure the name of the villa was in the picture, too.

'And one of you for the record?' Greg suggested to David. He didn't look very happy at the idea but gave a shrug and Greg took the picture, then, as David drove them back to town, Greg sent the pictures to the Buzzards, as he called them.

'Technology's great, isn't it?' Amy said happily. Things seemed to be working out at last, despite the fact that her father was still not with them. She had no doubt he would be returning home very soon, probably flying first class with his ill-gotten gains, she mused.

Was it so terrible? After all, the new drug may help some people, it was only her principles on poverty that were being offended. But she also felt certain that the poor tribes in South America were being exploited. If this herb was so rare and only grew in one secluded place, what would they do without it when it was all taken from them?

There were so many things that were still unanswered . . . like, how had the señor known they were coming to fetch their things?

'What are your plans now?' David asked as they arrived back in town.

'I think we'll probably fly home as soon as possible,' Amy told him. 'There's nothing more we can achieve by staying here.'

'I'll I drop you by your car, then. Good luck.'

They returned to their hire car and dumped their luggage, and Greg decided he needed more food.

'We can decide what we want to do next while we eat.'

'I shall be as fat as a pig if we eat this much this often,' groaned Amy after eating most of her pizza.

'Don't you want the rest of that?' Greg said, eyeing her plate.

'I don't know where you put it,' Amy commented, laughing. 'Whatever it is in your genes that lets you eat that much and stay so skinny,, you should synthesise it, market it and make your fortune.'

As she spoke she stared at him. This was so close to what her father had been doing, wasn't it? Maybe it wasn't so bad after all. Some people, like Greg, could eat vast quantities of food and never put on weight, while others piled on pounds and were on constant diets.

'I've been thinking. Maybe these drugs aren't all bad — it's just that the money is being made by the wrong people.' She explained her thoughts to Greg and he nodded.

'I'm glad you're not harbouring bad thoughts about your father. He might make things difficult for us after we're married.'

There was a moment's stunned silence.

'What did you say?' she stammered.

Greg repeated his words.

'This is a bit sudden, isn't it?' she squeaked. 'And when exactly are we getting married?' she asked incredulously.

'As soon as it can be arranged, actually.'

'And was I going to be asked for my opinion?'

'I'll let you choose the church. And your dress, of course. Oh . . . am I supposed to do the 'down-on-one knee' bit?'

'It might be nice,' she admitted.

So, in the middle of the busy lunchtime crowd, Greg knelt on the floor and asked Amy to marry him. She felt tears rising and swallowed hard.

'I didn't know you could be so romantic!' she murmured. 'Yes, please. I'd be so happy to marry you. But do get up.'

'I can't,' he groaned. 'My foot's really

painful. I'm stuck.'

She managed to haul him back on to his chair. There was a ripple of applause from the surrounding tables, and a waiter arrived with a bottle of Cava.

'With our compliments,' he said, producing two glasses.

'Thank you. That's really kind.'

'It is usually the evening when such proposals are made. I am sorry that we do not have the customary rose to present to you, señorita.'

'This is fine, thank you,' Amy replied, blushing to the roots of her hair. The waiter bowed and left them.

'This is all very embarrassing. How's your foot now?'

'Painful, actually. I'd forgotten about it in the adrenaline rush, but I'm not sure I can drive. How about we stay here for another day or two? While we wait for your father to join us.'

She pulled a face. 'I'd rather move somewhere else. We could drive a little way along the coast maybe, have a bit of a holiday before we go back. But what about work? Don't you have to get back?'

'They'll manage without me for a bit longer. Besides, I want to spend some time with my new fiancée — my new *official* fiancée, that is!'

It seemed strange to feel relaxed after the past few days. They wandered around the little towns and villages along the coast, gradually making their way towards the airport, until, after two whole days spent enjoying themselves, they felt it was time to move on.

'I think we should return home tomorrow,' Amy suggested.

'OK. Shall we send our Buzzard message and see if they can organise flight tickets?' Greg returned.

The call came back complete with a time for check-in, eleven o'clock the following morning.

'So tonight's our last night in Spain. Shall we find somewhere posh for a special dinner?'

'That would be nice. But tell me one thing — are our lives going to revolve round food and eating for ever? Because if they are, I'd better put in for some of Dad's new miracle drug!'

★ ★ ★

The following morning was wet. 'I thought it never rained here,' Greg grumbled. 'Are you ready?'

'Greg, I've been thinking . . . I'm not sure I *can* leave without Dad. I know he told us to go, but it just doesn't seem right.'

'So what do you want to do?'

'I guess there is only one thing to do,' she said, meeting his gaze.

'Go back to Mojácar? All right. I was pretty uneasy about it myself, to be honest. We'd better let the Buzzards know . . . '

They went through the now familiar routine with the phone.

'Look, I'm really sorry,' Amy began, 'but we can't leave Spain . . . '

' . . . without your father. Yes, I understand. But it's all right, there's been a development — your father is also en route to the airport.'

'What?' Amy squealed. 'You really mean it? How come?'

'We have terminated his work there. We have all the information we need and he is leaving. It will all be explained to you later. Now, hurry or you will miss your flight.'

With a sense of disbelief they drove to the airport and dropped off the car at the hire company's office there.

'It must have cost you a fortune. I'll make it up to you when Dad gets home,' Amy promised. 'We owe you heaps.'

'Don't worry about it. I wonder what we do about our tickets? I assume we go to the check-in desks and give them that booking ref the Buzzards gave you. I wonder where your dad is?'

Amy looked around but there was no sign of him.

'Shall we just check in anyway?' she began, but at that a voice called to them and they swung round.

'Dad!' She flung herself at him and

they hugged for several moments while Greg stood by awkwardly, not wanting to intrude.

Jeremy told them he had already checked in, so Greg and Amy went through the process, and it was only once they were through passport control and heading for their gate that Jeremy spoke up.

'Actually, love, I'm on a different flight,' he said. 'I have to go to London first. To check in with the office and give them some stuff from the señor. But I'll be home very soon.'

'But . . . '

'Go on — look, you're already being boarded. I'll be with you soon. It's all going to work out, I promise.'

'But, Dad, I don't . . . '

'Come on, love. Let's do as he says,' Greg said as he took her elbow and propelled her towards the gate. She looked back once to see her father blowing her a kiss, and then he was lost in the crowds.

'Does this mean the señor and the

Buzzards are working together? So why all the warnings to begin with? The comments about not being able to help us if we needed it? All that security?' Amy fretted.

'I suspect it was all to make sure we really did come out here.'

'You mean, they wanted to make sure we were suitably worried about it all? The security bit was probably just a game — they must have known I thought my father worked for the Government. It was all to ensure we were following their wishes.'

'Maybe. And I suppose I just complicated the issue by tagging along. Still, something good came out of it. We got together. But I still don't understand why it was necessary to lock us in, if your father was co-operating with it all along?'

'I don't think he was at first. I think maybe he was brought here against his better judgement. He must have got wind of something before, and that's why he wanted to make a new will

287

and left me the cryptic message on the magazine. It all seems a bit melodramatic, but it's the only explanation I can come up with.'

'But why all this stuff in Spain? Why couldn't he just continue to work at home?' Greg wondered.

'I don't know. I'm just speculating wildly here.'

'OK. So, home now or stay on?'

'Let's go home. Dad's on his way back anyhow. At least your parents will be pleased to see us.'

'And they'll be chuffed at our news. Especially my mum.' He laughed. 'Oh, I do love you, Amy Poolley.'

'And I love you, Greg.'

★ ★ ★

At eight o'clock that evening, they at last turned into the driveway of Greg's home. He opened the door and called out, 'Anyone home?'

Pamela and Henry came rushing out of the lounge.

'Goodness! Why on earth didn't you let us now you were coming? I haven't got a meal ready or anything. Are you all right? We were so worried about you. And where's Jeremy? Is he all right?'

'Whoa, Mum, one question at a time! We didn't know we were coming till the last minute. We ate on the flight. We're both fine. Jeremy's had to go straight to London ... Have I missed out anything?'

'Is he all right?'

'Fine when we left him this morning.'

'It's good to see you both,' Henry said quietly. 'You're looking well. Caught the sun, I see. So, you had a nice holiday?'

'Mixed.' Amy spoke for the first time. 'Very good in places,' she added, smiling at Greg.

'We got engaged, by the way,' Greg told them.

'Congratulations!' Henry said, pumping his son's hand. 'We couldn't be more pleased, could we, dear?'

Pamela was wiping away a tear. 'It's

the perfect ending. Now, come on, let's sit down and you can tell us everything.'

'It's a very long story,' Greg began. 'We didn't meet our contact till the second morning. Then it all began to go wrong . . . '

Pamela shook her head. 'I mean about your engagement! When did he propose and when are you getting the ring? Have you fixed the date yet?'

It was near to midnight before they finally finished telling the whole story. Amy had confided her concerns to Henry, though omitting her doubts about the integrity of the whole business. She was clinging to the words that her father had whispered a couple of days ago. 'Trust me'.

'Have you got any dirty washing?' Pamela asked, ever practical. 'I can put the washer on overnight and it'll all be ready for you tomorrow.'

'That would be great,' Amy agreed. 'If I had to wear these trousers for one more day, they'd get up and walk by themselves!'

* * *

As she lay in bed later, Amy reflected on what had happened since she'd last been here. It seemed like a strange dream, and there was a sense of anticlimax now. She felt almost sad that the excitement was over. How strange!

She finally fell asleep and slept peacefully until late the next day.

After breakfast, she wanted to go back to her own home.

'But you'll stay here with us until things are finally resolved?' Pamela pressed. 'Or at least until Jeremy comes back. I wouldn't be happy if you stayed in that big house on your own.'

'I would be all right, but I will stay on with you, if you don't mind. I still feel pretty unsettled.'

'Good. We can have some good old wedding gossip.'

'It's a bit soon for all that. We've made no plans yet.'

She did at least manage to spend the morning alone at home, as she'd hoped.

Greg was busy at his computer, tying to catch up on his own work. Henry had gone to give a lecture, and Pamela was busy cooking mountains of food to celebrate their return.

Her father's house seemed musty and she flung the windows open all round. The telephone messages were flashing away and she played them all. There seemed to be nothing important, but she made some notes, and then went on to list all the things that needed attention around the house. There was a heap of mail but nothing that looked important.

Before she left again, she checked that she'd closed all the windows, and put a new tape in the answering machine so that all the earlier messages would be ready for her father to deal with when he came back.

Pamela was in the kitchen alone when Amy returned to Greg's home. The girl decided to seize the moment.

'Can I ask you about my mother?' she said hesitantly. 'Nobody has ever talked about her much since I was old enough to understand.'

'I see.' Pamela hesitated, and then began to talk.

'Your mother was suffering from very severe post-natal depression. She loved you very much but she couldn't cope. When she told us *her* mother had been taken ill and she was going to stay with her and leave you here, with us, we — well, we thought it was a bit of an excuse. Your father was away on one of his trips — he should never have gone, but he did. Anyway, your grandmother was ill, and in fact died very quickly, and that was the final straw for your mother. In some sort of daze she went wandering out of the house and — well, she walked in front of a bus and was killed instantly.'

'That's just awful!' Amy was stunned. Such a tragedy!

'She was very confused, and I don't think anyone understood how bad she was feeling. Beautiful baby, happy marriage, a lovely home and a good life

— why should she have felt bad? People didn't understand post natal depression back then. Of course, we were all heart-broken. Your father lived with a deep sense of guilt. He engaged a nanny to look after you, and we did what we could to make you feel loved.'

'Thank you for telling me, Pamela, and for all you've done for me.'

They hugged with a new, deeper understanding. Amy was about to gain one very special mother-in-law.

They were sitting down to dinner that evening when there was a loud thump at the door and the bell was rung energetically.

'What on earth?' Henry said as he rose to his feet to open it.

'Heavens!' the others heard him exclaim. 'Where did you spring from?'

'Any room at the table for another?' boomed Jeremy, coming into the room. He grabbed Amy in a big hug and then greeted everyone else. 'It's good to see you all. I guessed this was where you must be when I found our house in darkness and the car gone. Lucky I'd kept the taxi, eh?'

'Is everything all right, Dad?' Amy asked with a tremor in her voice.

'I'm fine. Starving, but otherwise fine.'

'So, how were things left in Spain?' Greg asked. 'You weren't held any longer than necessary?' he pressed.

'Certainly not.'

'And Señor Parra-Mareno? He was really all right about you leaving?' Amy asked.

'I think so. I know you want to know all about it. I'll tell you when Pamela has given me a portion of her wonderful lasagne.'

He ate hungrily while the rest of them pretended to finish their own meals, impatient for explanations.

'That's better,' he said at last. 'Well, it all began a month or so ago ... My office had some information about a company headed by our friend Ignacio. He'd been doing dodgy deals around the world, primarily in South America.

He had paid for access to an area of rainforest and sent in his people to search out some of the herbs and ancient Indian medications he'd heard about. Posing as a pharmaceutical company, my office set up links with scientists whom Ignacio was enticed to use to develop his drugs, and they decided I should be sent there to work on it. Naturally suspicious, Ignacio wanted insurance to ensure of my loyalty and sent for you. I tried to warn you but they snatched the phone away.

'Greg put a spoke in the works when he decided to come with you, I can tell you, but eventually I convinced Ignacio that he could trust me.

'When Greg made his escape, Ignacio wanted to be sure the police weren't suspicious, so I played along with them so that you weren't locked up any longer. He was mildly surprised that you managed to escape too, Amy, and his men spent some hours trying to work out how you'd managed it. I don't think they ever did, actually!

'Once the work was finished, my office sent in another operative who had been working on the chemical side, and we gave Ignacio falsified reports. He hasn't realised that yet. However, he decided that I could leave — and here I am.'

'But what about all these riches you were promised? And the exploitation of the poor Indians?'

'That's the nice part. The so-called wonder slimming drug is dead in the water. The synthetic version is unstable and will never work, but he still thinks it will. I managed to insist that the right to collect the herbs was restored to the Indians. They'll probably make a decent living out of them, even if they're virtually useless to our friend. And my share of the loot is to go to the tribes and towards saving the rainforest. He thinks I'm potty, but I'm delighted that it's all behind me. Any pudding, Pam?'

'I'm not sure you deserve any, leading our children into such danger. If I'd known, I'd never have let them go.'

'So, what's going to happen to all the work you did?' Amy wondered.

'Nothing. I managed to convince them that I had done everything possible. They don't realise yet that I conned them into thinking it might work. Nobody would ever licence the drugs for use.'

'Pity, some people might have benefitted. Those of us with the sort of metabolism that copes with mountains of food can rarely sympathise enough with the rest of the world. How about another helping of your pie, Mum?' Greg said, ready to pour on extra cream.

'I just hope they don't send someone after you,' Henry said.

'My office will make sure that Ignacio and his colleagues are all discredited. He'll probably keep a very low profile for the next few years. He owns a dodgy fortune already and will want to make sure he keeps it.'

The conversation seemed to go on for hours but at last Greg took Amy's hand and led her outside.

'I just want to make sure we really are engaged, now we're back home and the adventure's all over. Do you really want to marry me?' he asked.

'Yes, please,' she whispered, and he took her in his arms and held her close.

'You two all right out there?' Pam called from the doorway.

'Just planning our wedding,' Greg called back wickedly.

'Well, come back in and let us hear exactly what you're planning. We want a proper ceremony. None of this slinking off somewhere in secret.'

'As if . . . ' Greg laughed.

'I love you, Greg,' Amy told him. 'And I don't care where we get married, just as long as it's very soon. I've been waiting all my life for this. I just didn't realise it before.'

We do hope that you have enjoyed reading this large print book.

Did you know that all of our titles are available for purchase?

We publish a wide range of high quality large print books including:
Romances, Mysteries, Classics
General Fiction
Non Fiction and Westerns

Special interest titles available in large print are:
The Little Oxford Dictionary
Music Book, Song Book
Hymn Book, Service Book

Also available from us courtesy of Oxford University Press:
Young Readers' Dictionary
(large print edition)
Young Readers' Thesaurus
(large print edition)

For further information or a free brochure, please contact us at:
Ulverscroft Large Print Books Ltd.,
The Green, Bradgate Road, Anstey,
Leicester, LE7 7FU, England.
Tel: (00 44) **0116 236 4325**
Fax: (00 44) **0116 234 0205**

Other titles in the
Linford Romance Library:

PALE ORCHID

Mavis Thomas

Bethany delays her hopes of rescuing a failing relationship while she helps a friend by working at The Corner Cattery. But there are unexpected problems. She becomes involved with twin brothers and the bitter feud between them: Dominic the successful but troubled and moody playwright; Darryl the dedicated doctor torn between his work in Africa and his two motherless children. Many conflicts must be resolved, and searching questions answered, before Bethany can see clearly her road ahead.

THE SEASONS OF LOVE

Zelma Falkiner

Stephanie laughed off warnings of summer holiday love affairs. She was quite sure she could resist the famed beauty and passion of Greece, and concentrate on her new job as tour leader of a group of Australians. It isn't a handsome Greek who steals her heart, but an Englishman named William Brown. But is he who he says he is? And, more importantly for her, is it the wrong season for a long-lasting romance?

JUST ONE LOOK

Joan Reeves

When Jennifer Moore sees her new physician, she grabs her clothes and flees in her skimpy paper gown. When did Matt Penrose become a doctor? How could he not recognize her? She's never forgotten him and his teasing about her newly developed figure in high school. Matt's comeuppance is long overdue. It's Jennifer's turn to tease him this time around. The baffled doctor can't figure her out, but she's too lovely to resist. And hasn't he seen her somewhere before?

SUNLIGHT ON SHADOWS

Pat Posner

Rissa leaves Foxleigh and her only remaining family, when she hears that Logan, her late brother's best friend, is in love with her widowed sister-in-law. When she returns four years later, even though she's engaged to Justin, Rissa is distraught to discover how wrong she's been about Logan — who is now living in Ireland. When Rissa's secret doubts about Justin are confirmed and Logan returns, it's perfectly clear he still sees Rissa as a sort of sister . . . isn't it?